GUNSMOKE IS GREY

The doctor told O'Brien he'd have to rest up for a couple of months before he could strap his Colt back on. Still, he had to earn a living, and he was grateful to the doc when he gave him a nice, quiet job across the territory. O'Brien and his new partner found a town in fear and a hardcase who would stop at nothing to get what he wanted. Although he was in no shape to take on the bully-boys, when it came to curing the problem at Rock View, O'Brien knew the prescription was simple—lead, lead and more lead.

GUNSMOKE IS GREY

GUNSMOKE IS GREY

by
Ben Bridges

Dales Large Print Books
Long Preston, North Yorkshire,
England.

British Library Cataloguing in Publication Data.

Bridges, Ben
    Gunsmoke is grey.

    A catalogue record for this book is
    available from the British Library

    ISBN 1-85389-758-2 pbk

First published in Great Britain by Robert Hale Ltd., 1996

Copyright © 1994 by David Whitehead

Cover illustration © FABA by arrangement with Norma
Editorial SA

The right of David Whitehead to be identified as the author
of this work has been asserted by him in accordance with
the Copyright, Designs and Patents Act, 1988

Published in Large Print 1997 by arrangement with Robert
Hale Ltd.

Dales Large Print is an imprint of
Library Magna Books Ltd.
Printed and bound in Great Britain by
T.J. International Ltd., Cornwall, PL28 8RW.

For Laurie Robinson

ONE

O'Brien rode into Purgatory thinking, *Wonder how long I've got before the shooting starts?*

He came in off the high desert aboard a snug-muscled little mustang, riding easy in his Texas double-rig and trailing a spare saddle-mount beside him. A dry, warm wind followed him in from the east, sending dust-devils spiralling up the street ahead of him and making the lamps suspended at regular intervals from porch overhangs sway drunkenly back and forth.

Midway down the single street he drew in and slowly looked up. As the brim of his tobacco-brown Stetson tilted back, his face was revealed in the poor yellow light. It was strong and whiskery, tanned and weathered, with a smallish nose and a generous mouth and eyes that were very pale blue.

Night was already three or four hours old, and the wide Utah sky above was clear and grainy with stars. Most of the cabins around him were in darkness, but the larger, sturdier building at the far end of the street—Habgood's, according to the sign over the door—was blazing with light and noise; a squeeze-box and fiddle, the odd yell and squeal of men and women enjoying themselves, the constant clink of bottleneck on glass-rim.

Purgatory, he thought with a wry shake of the head. A place of torment and suffering. Except that it didn't sound like there was too much suffering going on at the moment.

He eyed his surroundings critically. Officially, Purgatory did not exist. And, to be honest, you couldn't call the half-dozen or so shacks that ran along either side of the worn trail a real town. It was more what you might term a sanctuary. An outlaw sanctuary.

O'Brien brushed himself down. An accumulation of dust and dried salt powdered the man and his horses. He had been on the trail a week, after a fellow called McManus told him he would more than likely find his quarry here. And McManus should know. He ran a trading post on the other side of the Great Salt Lake Desert and was widely considered by members of the bounty hunting fraternity to be 'in the know'. The man O'Brien was looking for had a woman there, he explained. Well, whore, really, name of Polly Parker.

O'Brien had asked for a description of the girl and got it. But then, once he'd spilled coins into McManus' palm and turned to toe into the stirrup, the trading post proprietor had added a warning. 'You're a dead man if you ride into Purgatory, O'Brien. Them folks up there, they look after their own. You make an enemy of one, you make an enemy of 'em *all.*'

O'Brien weighed that but didn't really believe it. He'd spent years locking horns with badmen of every stripe, and very few of them adhered to any true code of honour.

Still, he couldn't deny that he was running a hell of a risk. He was a fighting man by trade, and though he was by no means the only man who ever hired out his gun, he was most certainly among the best, quite possibly *the* best. Over the years he had made his living doing the things other men said couldn't be done. And in between times, when his bankroll grew lean, he had hunted bounty.

Maybe some of the men he had hunted in the past were here now, in Purgatory. Maybe they would recognise him when he finally entered Habgood's. Maybe, if he was lucky, he would make his collar smooth and quiet and get his man out of town before the fellow's cronies were any the wiser.

Or maybe all hell would bust loose the minute he stepped through the door and he would go down in a sudden burst of gunfire and they would bury him here in this outlaw stronghold where, according to McManus, even federal lawmen dared not come.

He thought about all of that, about the

long, hard journey he had made across the sun-blasted desert, with its endless vista of sagebrush and shad scale and dried-up juniper trees, a bitch of a journey he would have to make back the other way with his prisoner in tow, and wondered if it was worth all the risk.

Then he thought about his quarry.

Omaha Tom Barfoot had deserted from the US Army in late '78 and dropped completely out of sight for six months until a man answering his description was involved in a bank robbery down in Colorado. He'd gotten away with about fifty thousand dollars'-worth of non-negotiable securities and left a gut-shot bystander to die in the dirt following a brief gunfight. Three months later he was involved in an attempted bank robbery that ended with the murder of a local justice of the peace. In the next seven years he took part in eight bank robberies, four attempted bank robberies, four train hold-ups and at least two stagecoach robberies. Along the way he killed seven men that the authorities knew about, and was implicated in the murder of at least four more. It was estimated that his life of crime had netted him close to ninety thousand dollars, although O'Brien was sceptical about that. Still, it must have come to a fair piece, because the reward on him had recently notched up to an impressive five thousand dollars, payable whether Tom was alive or dead.

He reached up, unbuttoned his wolfskin jacket and drew his .38 Colt Lightning from leather, then checked the action and loads. Moonlight spilled molten silver along the three and one-half inch rounded barrel. At last, satisfied that the gun would be as reliable as ever if it came to shooting, he slipped it away and heeled the mustang back into motion. As they went deeper into the town that was not a town at all, headed for the big saloon, he briefly reviewed in his mind the wanted dodger that had brought him here, seeing again the passable sketch of Omaha Tom's ugly-looking, brutish face.

He saw thick, shaggy black hair tumbling down over the simian slope of Tom's forehead, his surly dark gaze, the badly-healed break running left to right across the line of his nose, his thick, twisted lips and square, stubbly jaw. He saw a man aged beyond his forty years, aged and corrupted and rendered somehow less than human by all the crimes he had committed.

He approached the saloon at a walk, providing the only movement in an otherwise deserted street. A few horses were standing hipshot at the tie-rack out front. To the left and a little behind the place was a pen in which more horses milled aimlessly. Saddles formed a hill-and-hollow line along the top rail, cinch-straps hanging groundward like a collection of dead snakes.

He drew rein and swung down outside the saloon and tied both his mount and the spare animal at the rail there. He didn't figure on staying long enough to make off-saddling worthwhile, and in any case, it could be that he'd need to make a fast getaway.

He paused for a moment, standing tall, six feet one or two, with the slim, compact build of a man born to the saddle. He didn't want to keep thinking about all the things that could go wrong in the next few minutes, it might jar his concentration, but it was as well to prepare for any eventuality. That was how he'd stayed alive this long. After a moment he pulled in a deep breath and licked his lips, then started up onto the porch and across to the door.

It opened just as he got there and two big men pushed out into the darkness and went to hunt up their horses. Tugging at his hat-brim, O'Brien said, ''Evenin'.'

They glanced up at him. His stomach clenched. But though he was a newcomer, he saw no flicker of suspicion in their eyes, only lack of interest and perhaps a tacit kind of acceptance. No doubt they felt safe here, among their own kind and secure in the knowledge that the law, even the dubious law of the bounty hunter, did not extend to this isolated northwestern section of the territory. They returned his nod, then went to cut their horses out of the pen.

O'Brien watched them go, releasing a long, slow breath. So far, he thought, so good. Again he wondered if anyone inside would recognise him from some past encounter. The beard he had allowed to grow over the past week would disguise his features a bit. But would that be enough?

There was only one way to find out.

He twisted the door-handle and went inside.

The saloon was long and low and crowded. Pausing a moment as he closed the door behind him, he surveyed the place through a grey haze of tobacco-smoke.

About thirty tables had been crammed into the sawdusted space between the left-side wall and the plank-and-barrel counter opposite. Behind the bar, three men in their late thirties or early forties could hardly dispense cheer fast enough to please a crowd that stood three deep in places. O'Brien ran his eyes across the patrons and saw men who were tall or short, fat or thin, dark or fair, young or old, and some who were curiously young and old all in one. Lamplight cast ruddy cones down over the proceedings as he watched them eat or drink or dance with the scattering of shrew-faced, disease-riddled whores. It was hot in Habgood's place, stifling almost, as he listened to the slap of playing cards on wood, the occasional explosion of bawdy laughter, the constant buzz of chatter and the diamondback-rattle of busy dice-shakers.

He pushed through the throng towards the bar and managed to elbow himself to the front of the crowd. Over in the far corner, a thin man in a grey shirt and black pants and a fiddle stuck under his chin seemed to be having a conniption fit, but judging from all the toe-tapping going on, his efforts were obviously meeting with the approval of his equally-enthusiastic audience.

One of the bartenders spotted him and raised his eyebrows questioningly. He was fat and sweating, with heavily-greased black hair and a beard, and sausages for fingers. 'What'll it be?' he asked.

O'Brien asked for whiskey. The bartender poured it into a smeared shot-glass and said, 'Dollar.'

O'Brien eyed him sidelong. 'Kind of expensive, isn't it?'

The beard split with a cold grin. 'So go elsewhere.'

They both knew there wasn't anywhere else, so O'Brien paid up and moved away. He drifted through the crowd, keeping his eyes peeled for Barfoot and nursing the drink to make it last, but after five minutes of careful, covert observation, he decided Barfoot wasn't there to be seen.

With the smooth ease of long practice, a red-headed percenter with a painted smile and a wall eye wrapped herself around his free arm and said, 'Like to buy a lonely gal some champagne, honey?'

He glanced down at her. She was underfed and tired-looking, twenty going on fifty. The attempt she made to look alluring was pathetic. He said, 'Not tonight, Josephine,' and made to slip out of her grip, but she said, 'How'd you know my name was Josephine?'

He looked at her again, closer this time. He knew her name wasn't anything like Josephine. But for a dollar she would be anything he wanted her to be. She was such a sad little figure, so desperate to please, that it might not even cost that much. After a moment he shrugged and decided to humour her. 'I don't know. You *look* like a Josephine.'

Her eyelashes fluttered. 'I *do?*'

'Sure.' An idea occurred to him. 'Say, Jo—I'm looking for Polly Parker. Is she around tonight?'

The girl's painted mouth thinned down jealously. 'Oh, *her.*'

'Is she around?'

She put a hand on one spare hip. 'What's she got that I haven't?' she asked.

'Nothing,' he said. 'It's just that she's my sister.'

That mollified her somewhat. 'Oh. Well. That's different, I guess.' She gestured to a doorless aperture in the rear wall that was covered by an old, plain blue curtain. 'Second room on the left.'

'Thanks.'

''Course,' she said, striving to be diplomatic. 'This might not be the best time to disturb her, iffen you know what I mean.'

He played a hunch. 'You mean she's with Tom?'

She nodded.

He felt a sudden surge of satisfaction, excitement, apprehension. 'Well,' he assured her, 'don't you worry your pretty little head about that, petal. I'm kind of looking forward to seeing Tom again, too.'

He took a pace away from her but she said, 'Hey.'

Trying to hide his impatience, he said, 'What?'

'Do you *really* think I look like a Josephine?' she asked, almost shyly. 'Josephine's a beautiful name.'

He looked into her face. She had a bloodless, almost translucent skin and it was pulled taut over her cheekbones and forehead. A scattering of freckles showed just above the meagre swell of her breasts, as did her ribs. She was washed up, washed out, probably a little slow in the brain.

But it was her eyes that told him more about her than anything else. O'Brien looked into them and almost forgot why he had come here in the first place, because they spoke so eloquently of sadness and disappointment and a pitiful desire just to please, and to be wanted and valued because of it.

He found the sudden flash of insight distracting and thus unwelcome. He was here to do a job, a hard and maybe violent job, not dispense charity. But, hell, a little kindness wouldn't cost anything.

After a while he nodded. 'Sure you look like a Josephine,' he said, adding for the hell of it, 'Name suits you.'

She'd been holding her breath. Now she released it in a rush, and when she smiled it was the real thing this time, not the painted greeting reserved for customers. 'Oh. Well,' she said again, curiously and appealingly coy, 'I...I guess I'd better let you run along.'

'I'd appreciate it.'

'See you later, maybe?'

'Maybe.'

He held out what was left in the shot-glass. 'Here,' he said. 'You might as well finish this off.'

He could have been offering her a diamond ring from the way she accepted it, all saucer-eyed and round-mouthed in surprise. That was how used to kindness she was.

'Say, thanks.'

He moved away from her, heading for the stained curtain she had indicated with his pulses hammering. He brushed the drape aside and entered a narrow, dim passageway with two doors opening off each side wall.

Quickly he scanned his new surroundings, cursing softly because there was no back way out. Light showed in a thin yellow strip at the bottom of the second door to his left. Near as he could tell, the other rooms were in darkness, though that didn't necessarily mean to say they were empty.

He crossed to Polly Parker's door, moving as quiet as a shadow across peach-fuzz and willing the boards underfoot to hold firm and not betray him with a creak. Once there, he put an ear to one of the thin panels. He could guess well enough what Omaha Tom and his lady love were doing in there, but it would make his job considerably easier if he could get a rough idea whereabouts in the room they were doing it.

The curtain did a little to muffle all the sounds coming at him from the bar-room beyond, but not enough. A moment passed and then he gave a mental curse, because he couldn't hear a thing. He stood back, thinking, *Well, you can't have everything.* At least there wasn't any lock on the door; that was something.

He cat-footed back to the curtain and peered out through one of its small tears, just to make sure he wasn't about to be disturbed. Since saloon life was continuing a-pace, he went back to the Parker room door and drew his .38.

A single bead of sweat oozed from one temple and slid down his cheek as he reached his free hand down to the door handle, closed palm and fingers around it and...

He went in there fast, knowing he had to take charge at once, before Tom could reach for his gun or Polly could voice a scream. Almost before they realised it, he had slipped nimbly into the room and closed the door with a soft click behind him.

His eyes were everywhere at once, gauging the room's mean dimensions, noting the position of the few paltry sticks of furniture, the whereabouts of its two inhabitants, and as they swung around to face him and the woman said, 'Who the hell—?', he raised the Lightning in his fist and said, 'Not a sound. Either of you.'

The woman had been fixing her face at the mirror atop the chest of drawers. There was no doubt in O'Brien's mind that she was Polly Parker, for McManus had described her well. It was difficult to estimate her age. Her skin was chalky with rice-powder and her mouth was a jarring crimson slash, while the high colour in her gaunt cheeks owed more to the over enthusiastic application of rouge than anything else. She was a lot of woman, he thought, all bust and backside, with curly auburn hair and long, dangling earrings that reflected and diffused the light of the Argant lamp on the bedside cabinet, throwing her shadow up the wall to join all the other shadows gathered on the ceiling.

Tom Barfoot had been stretched out on the bed, stripped down to his red Balbriggans with a brown-paper cigarette dangling from his mouth. Now he was coming up off the mattress with a jolt, spitting out the quirley and automatically rolling sideways to reach down for the butt of the .45 protruding from the weapons belt coiled on the floor beside him.

O'Brien didn't even pause for breath. He crossed the room in two long strides and brought his foot down hard on Omaha Tom's questing fingers. Tom said something like, *'Awcris'thathurt!'* and withdrew his hand fast, glaring daggers at O'Brien as he kicked the gunbelt across the floor out of reach and himself backed up towards the far end of the room to join it.

Tom rubbed his hand. His expression was that of a petulant child. But small fires had ignited in his dark brown eyes. Although he looked to be a bit shorter than O'Brien had imagined, the sketch of him on the wanted dodger was actually a pretty fair likeness. He really was as ugly as the artist had made him out to be. The only thing missing was the ruddy, hot-looking flush to his skin and the fine sheen of sweat on his sloping forehead, showing like silver now in the dismal lamplight.

O'Brien put his back against the door, his expression betraying nothing of the tension that was heightening his every sense. He said, 'Get up, Barfoot. Slowly. And get dressed.'

Licking his lips, Omaha Tom regarded him cautiously. 'An' who're you?' he asked at length, attempting a show of bravado.

O'Brien said, 'Can't you guess?'

Tom shrugged. He had big arms and thick legs and a belly just loosening up and turning to blubber. 'The law?'

O'Brien shook his head. 'What comes *before* the law.'

Understanding came into Tom's expression, along with disgust. 'A bounty hawk,' he said.

The room was claustrophobic and cheerless. O'Brien had the best reason in the world not to tarry there any longer than he could help. 'Get dressed,' he said again.

'Now wait a minute, mister. I don't know who the hell you think you are, bustin' in here like this, but I can tell you this for sure—whoever you think I am, I *ain't*. Understan' me? You got yourself the wrong man.'

O'Brien's lips twitched briefly and his eyes grew flat like a snake's. 'Don't play me for a fool, Tom. I haven't got the time. Just do like I say. And no tricks.'

Omaha Tom studied him for a moment. The man he saw looked tough and determined. Maybe he was prepared to use the gun in his hand and maybe he wasn't. Tom couldn't really say for sure. But tough and determined though he might be, they didn't come any more determined than Omaha Tom Barfoot.

With a shrug he reached for his clothes, which had been hurriedly discarded on the chair at the foot of the bed. 'You won't get away with this,' he prophesised calmly, putting his arms into the sleeves of his shirt and then shrugging it over his shaggy head. 'Not lessen you brought an army with you.'

Before he could make any kind of response to that, O'Brien heard voices outside, a man and a woman, and tensed. The door just across the passage opened and closed. The sound increased his sense of urgency. 'Hurry it up, there,' he hissed.

Tom regarded him with a smirk. 'Look at you,' he said. 'A big man with a gun in his hand. But you could save yourself a whole lot of grief if you'd only use your head.'

'Oh? How's that?'

Tom looked up at him. 'Suppose for a minute I *am* whoever it is you came here to collar,' he said. 'How much am I worth these days?'

When O'Brien told him he whistled, obviously surprised and impressed. 'All right,' he said after a moment. 'Five thousand dollars. It's yours. I'll *give* it to you. All you got to do in return is pretend you never found me. Sound reasonable?'

Silence filled the room. Polly stared from one man to the other. 'It's a hell of an easier way to pick up your blood money than what *you* got planned,' Tom said persuasively. 'An' no risks.'

O'Brien said, 'Just the risk I'd be taking if I was fool enough to trust you,' and shook his head. 'No—I'll collect my money from the marshal's office in Brigham, if it's all the same to you.'

Tom's face hardened and the fires in his eyes burned down to embers. 'Then you're a dead man, mister,' he said quietly.

'That's enough gab,' O'Brien replied, unmoved. 'Finish dressing.'

Tom's response was an insolent grin. But at last he sat down on the bed and hauled on his scuffed Justins and tucked his grey pants into them. He didn't look like a man who'd made much money from crime. But then, men like Tom never held onto the money long enough for it to make a difference. Once he was through pulling on his boots, he stood up and said, 'All right. I'm dressed. Now what?'

'We're walking out of here,' O'Brien replied, shucking his jacket and draping it over his right arm in such a way to disguise the fact that he was holding a gun in his hand. 'I've got horses out front. We're going to walk right out like two old friends, and then we're going to mount up and ride.'

The outlaw narrowed his eyes. 'You think I'm gonna help you take me in?'

'I *know* you are. Because if you don't, I'll put a bullet in you.'

He fixed Polly Parker with a stern eye. 'And you'd better remember that, Polly. Raise the alarm too soon after we've gone and I'll gut-shoot your lover-boy here at the first sign of pursuit.'

'An' risk losin' out on the reward?' she asked with a bitter twist to her painted lips.

He said, 'Sure, if there's any kind of

chance that I might not live long enough to collect it.'

His pale blue eyes bored right into her. It was crucial that she believe that he meant what he said and not to have sand enough to call his bluff. He looked into her eyes. It was difficult to read any emotion in them, but perhaps he saw just a little fear there, and uncertainty, and that was good.

'All right, Tom,' he said after a moment, reaching down to take the outlaw's gun from leather and jam it into his own presently-empty holster. 'Get your hat and coat.'

'You're never gonna make it, mister.'

'For your sake, you better pray that I do.'

Polly's lower lip trembled theatrically. 'Honey...'

'Aw, don't worry 'bout me, little sugar,' Tom said with a grin. 'It's a long way 'twixt here and civilisation. A lot can happen.'

O'Brien listened a moment at the door, heard nothing, just the muted sounds of revelry coming from the bar-room. 'All right,' he said, opening the door and motioning with his gun that Tom should precede him. 'Take it nice and easy. And remember. First sign of trouble and I burn you down.'

They looked at each other.

O'Brien said firmly, 'I mean it, Tom.'

He didn't know if Omaha Tom believed him or not. His expression was a miser; it gave nothing away. The outlaw pushed out through the curtain with O'Brien right beside him. At once the smoky, boozy, too-warm air slapped them in the face.

O'Brien quickly scanned the room. As far as he could see, their entrance had attracted little attention. He figured it was about a twenty-yard walk to the door. He knew for sure that it was going to be the longest twenty yards he'd ever walked in his life.

'Let's go,' he said.

They started shouldering through the crowd, side by side, O'Brien trying to keep his eyes on his prisoner and the men around them all at once. He hoped to hell that Tom believed what he'd said in warning. If he decided to call O'Brien's bluff and break away or yell for help, hell would bust loose in no uncertain terms. O'Brien didn't care to consider how many men might die if that happened.

The door was about fifteen yards away now, just the other side of a lazy gauze of tobacco smoke and whiskey fumes. O'Brien, walking gut-tight, thought about what lay beyond it; the horses, the cool, cloaking night air, the desert and, at the end of the trail, the town of Brigham, and five thousand dollars.

A card game reached its conclusion just as they passed it by, and the winner powered up out of his chair so fast that O'Brien's grip on the hidden handgun tightened dangerously. But all the fellow said was, 'Drinks're on me, boys! Hey, Habgood, let's have some more whiskey over here!'

O'Brien released his breath in a soft exhalation. This business was stringing him out tight as barbed wire. Maybe he was getting too old for it all. But they were just ten yards from the door, now. Thirty feet, that's all. Twenty eight, twenty six, twenty four...

Some weird, itchy feeling at the nape of his neck, a danger signal he had learned over the years to heed and heed well, made him glance a ways off to the left. A sparrow-chested man standing up at the bar in a grey jacket and check shirt was watching him with a frown on his long, seamed face. For just a moment their eyes locked, and then O'Brien looked away, his stomach lurching unpleasantly.

There was something about the man's narrow, sea-blue eyes, the curl of his iron-grey walrus moustache... He knew that face. He couldn't place it right away—he had other things on his mind just then—but he definitely knew it. And if he remembered that man, then that man might also remember him.

He and Tom continued walking. O'Brien thought about the man at the bar, tried to put a name to him. Fanshaw? Fanning? Falloway. That was it. Falloway. A road-agent. He'd been part of a gang raising stagecoaches down in the Big Bend country of Texas, sometime around '79 or '80. But that was better than five years ago. Long enough, O'Brien wondered, for Falloway to have forgotten the face of the man who'd finally arrested him?

He could hope. But the Falloway he recalled was just like all the rest of them, sour-tempered, a grudge-toter, a man who would always try to get even, no matter how long it took.

He could still feel the man's eyes upon him. But what had he seen in them? Idle curiosity? Suspicion? Recognition?

Beside him, Omaha Tom sensed that something had happened or was about to happen, that O'Brien's fine plan to walk him right out of there was about to come unstuck. He deliberately started to drag his heels. O'Brien moved his gunhand a fraction so that Tom would feel the barrel pressing into his kidneys, and said in an undertone, 'Keep going.'

He saw from the edge of his vision that Falloway had pushed away from the bar and was shoving through the crowd on a course that would intercept them before they could reach the door. They kept striding towards it anyway, with Falloway still ploughing steadily towards them. The door was only about twenty feet away now.

Eighteen...

Sixteen...

Fourteen...

Falloway opened his mouth and raised his voice, 'Hey, you...'

O'Brien wanted to curse his bad luck but knew that now was not the time. He was in a tight corner that was getting tighter all the while. But instinctively the professional in him took over and he started to plot the best course out of there if it should come to a shooting fight.

Falloway was no more than seven or eight feet away from them now. Again he said, 'Hey, you...'

O'Brien ignored him, concentrating solely on reaching the door even though he knew he wasn't going to make it. He saw the man closing on him rapidly, reaching out one hand to grasp him by the shoulder and swing him around—

But then he caught a flash of red and chanced a look around just as the girl he had spoken to earlier, the girl who had called herself Josephine, stepped deftly into Falloway's path, bringing him to a sudden halt, and snaked one of her thin arms through one of his.

O'Brien didn't wait to see what happened next. His priority now was just to make the most of the distraction the girl had provided and keep moving. He shoved Tom the last couple of feet to the door, opened it and prodded him out into the night, wondering if the girl had come to his aid deliberately. What other reason could she have had for blocking Falloway's path the way she had?

But there was no time to ponder that now. The clean, crisp air was good after the heady, stifling atmosphere of Habgood's. O'Brien indicated the spare saddle-horse at the rack and said, 'Mount up. Quickly, now.'

'Gettin' jumpy?' Tom asked sarcastically.

'You'll be the first to know about it if I am.'

O'Brien went around the rack and untethered the mustang, then threw his jacket up over the pommel and stepped up to leather. He didn't know how long Jo would be able to hold Falloway's attention, but even if it was just seconds, he had to make the most of them.

They peeled away from Habgood's place and O'Brien, never normally a one to count his chickens before they hatched, couldn't believe he might actually have pulled it off. A wind sprang up to blow more tiny spiralling dust-devils in off the desert, and the lanterns hung at regular intervals along the porch overhangs swayed and squeaked the spilled saffron light in uncertain arcs.

Just as they started to ride out of Purgatory, the door to Habgood's opened and Falloway charged out onto the porch and yelled, 'Hey, *you!*'

A woman's shrill scream sliced through the air at roughly the same moment, and though she was still out of sight inside the saloon, Polly Parker followed it with a damning indictment yelled at the top of her not-unimpressive lungs.

'*He's the law! He's taken my Tom! He's got Tom!*'

O'Brien swore under his breath. Looked like he'd been wrong about Polly. But hell, that was women for you.

Tom's eyes were on him. 'Give it up, mister,' he advised.

O'Brien glared at him. 'The hell you say!'

He reached over and slapped Tom's mount on the rump, and startled, the animal leapt into motion, almost unseating its rider as it tore off up the street.

A gunshot blasted through the night and O'Brien hunkered low over his mustang's muscly neck. Another gunshot sizzled through the darkness and men spilled out onto the porch, demanding to know what in hell was going on.

Suddenly Purgatory was the most inhospitable place on the face of the planet. Confusion was rife, but even so, O'Brien knew that these liquored-up, trigger-happy sons would be more inclined to shoot first and ask questions later. He jammed his heels into the mustang's flanks, but instead of bolting the horse reared up, confused and unnerved by the gunfire and unsure what to do for the best.

Falloway yelled, *'Get 'im!'*

Out in the middle of the street, as clear a target as any of them could have wished for, O'Brien fought his mount back down, and as it turned sideways on to the crowd pushing out of the saloon, he brought his .38 around on them and fired twice.

Flame spat through the night. As one, the men on the porch ducked low. But O'Brien wasn't interested in making a fight out of it. The odds were too damn' long for that.

Instead, his bullets found the lantern swaying gently at the far end of the overhang and it burst apart in a miniature eruption of flame, oil and splintering glass.

Even as fire rained down from heaven, it began to catch and spread across the dry, weathered wood of the porch, bringing renewed howls from the men crouching there. O'Brien snap-aimed at the lantern that mirrored it at the other end of the overhang and again his Colt cracked and the lantern burst apart.

Suddenly the porch was in uproar. O'Brien knew that if they caught him, there would be no punishment too cruel for these men to inflict upon him.

Therefore, they must not catch him.

He wheeled the mustang around and kicked it into motion. Behind him, the shouting men straightened up and, while some tried to stamp out the spreading fire, others ran for the saddled horses tugging at the rack or the animals milling, nervously now, in the pen.

O'Brien emptied the .38 as he blurred up the street after Omaha Tom, shooting out lanterns as he went. One after another they exploded and oil-fed flame splashed down over wood just ripe for the burning.

Mane flying wildly, muscles knotting and flexing, the mustang thundered on up the street. O'Brien stuffed the .38 into his belt, drew Tom's .45 and started on the lanterns hanging intact along the other side of the street.

Shattering glass added to the growing

42

cacophony. Twisted metal jolted and fell from hooks. Liberated flame spread swiftly across cabin and store-front alike. The night air began to stink of the smell of burning, the faint breeze began to spread it and waft smoke in a cloaking black-grey curtain between him and his would-be pursuers.

At the end of the street he dared to draw in and turn the heaving horse sideways on again in order to survey the damage. Smoke was billowing up towards the black, star-filled sky. Flames were alternately reaching out and then shrinking back, leaping nine, ten, a dozen feet into the air, licking greedily up and over the crude shacks. Above the roar he heard men yelling, something about fetching water, he thought, and that was good, because while they were fetching water, they wouldn't be chasing him.

He was just about to turn the horse away when a hastily-mounted rider burst through the wall of smoke with a sixgun in his hand. As O'Brien recognised Falloway's now-contorted face, Falloway's watering sea-blue eyes came to rest on him and he fired his gun twice in rapid succession.

Again O'Brien's mustang sidestepped nervously, but steeling himself against a natural impulse to dodge or duck, O'Brien brought Tom's .45 up and returned fire.

Falloway's horse broke stride and then stumbled a little sideways, and Falloway went backwards off the charging animal with a screech that ended in a gurgle when he connected with the ground.

But though he was down, he sure wasn't out. 'Fact, he was back on his feet almost at once, sixgun still bucking and blasting in his fist.

O'Brien, fighting his own prancing horse, clenched his teeth and fired back, and Falloway screamed as a red spray burst up and out ahead of him, and he dropped the gun, grabbed his torso and twisted sideways and down.

O'Brien looked at him, hunched up there and still as a stone, dyed red by the flames growing steadily around them.

A moment passed, but no-one else came through the smoke after him, so O'Brien turned the mustang and got out of there.

Up ahead, Omaha Tom was just getting the spare horse under control and thinking about turning it around and heading back into the burning town. O'Brien rode up and reined in to block his trail.

'Uh-huh,' he said.

Tom glared at him. Amber shadows danced wildly across his face. 'You won't get away with this,' he said in a low voice, his words almost drowned by the crackle and spit of the feeding flames.

'You already said that,' O'Brien reminded him.

'I mean it,' Tom growled sullenly. 'It's a long way 'twixt here an' Brigham, mister. Remember that. A lot can happen.'

O'Brien's eyes went flat again. The last twenty minutes had passed more like twenty years, and he wasn't out of the woods yet. 'Let's go,' he said, indicating the desert shelving away beneath the starlight ahead of them. 'And *you* remember something. You cause me any more grief before we reach Brigham and so help me, Tom, I'll have your balls for bed-knobs.'

TWO

They rode through the night, away from Purgatory, and in so doing they swapped one kind of hell for another.

The night was cold, like all desert nights, but the travelling was easier. Still, O'Brien kept one eye on their back-trail, just in case, but there was no pursuit, just a distant orange glow to mark the position of the outlaw town and the fire that threatened to consume it.

The night ticked away and hours later the sky began to streak with false dawn. A short time after that they spied the sun swelling up on the eastern horizon, and slowly, slowly, as the dark gave way to light, shadows began to form and pull back from the west to huddle beneath the rocks and brush that had cast them.

At length, the desert was revealed in its entirety.

46

The desert.

It was, like all deserts, hell with the flames out, a flat, endless wasteland of sand and salt grass, pickle weed and greasewood, and, on the surface at least, that was all. 'Far as the eye could see in every direction, there was just a deadening landscape beginning to quiver now as the air warmed up and began to thicken like jelly. Only the flies and spiders and scorpions felt at home there. Only the occasional juniper tree broke the monotony and offered the promise of scant shade when the day grew towards its hottest—about an hour or so after noon. But rain was an infrequent visitor to these parts, so the juniper grew mostly as shrub in the juiceless soil.

Years before, the railroad had decided to trend north and skirt around this no-man's-land rather than attempt to cross it. O'Brien had learned well over the past week why; because with the rising sun came the heat, pleasant at first, for it chased away the seeping coldness of the night. But then it began to build and

47

eventually hammer harshly at the men and their drooping mounts, and along towards noon O'Brien indicated a few trees about half a mile ahead and to the north and said, 'We'll hole up there for a while.'

Tom eyed him from out of a sweat-flushed face. 'It's about damn' time.'

They angled the horses towards the shade of prickle-pointed leaves and dismounted. Wordlessly they loosened their cinch-straps. O'Brien took off his hat, ran one hand up through his short, damp salt-and-pepper hair, then took one of the skins from around his saddlehorn and poured water into his hat, for the horses. Any man with a lick of sense always put care of his horse first, because without a horse in country like this, that man was as good as dead. Only when the animals had slaked their thirst did O'Brien pass the skin across to Omaha Tom.

The outlaw was as dry as dust, but knew better than to make a hog of himself. Water was a precious commodity in this land. As he passed the skin back to O'Brien he wiped a sleeve across his mouth and said, 'You got enough o' that to last us?'

'If we're careful with it,' O'Brien replied, taking a pull and swilling it around his mouth to shift the grit from his teeth.

'I hope to hell you're right. This ain't no land a-tall to develop a thirst in.'

'There's a sump about thirty miles from here. As long as we can make what we've got in these skins last till we reach it, we'll be all right.'

'What makes you think you'll *ever* reach it?' Tom asked, baiting him.

O'Brien only smiled. 'What makes *you* think that I won't?'

Tom made no reply, but he thought, *You gotta sleep sometime, don'tcha?*

He slumped down, put his back to a tree and closed his eyes. 'Man, oh man,' he said with feeling. 'I swear, I could sleep for a week.' And to prove it, he loosed off a jaw-cracker of a yawn.

'Get some shut-eye, then,' O'Brien invited. 'We won't be going any further now till the day cools down.'

He delved into his saddlebags and

brought out a couple of strips of smoke-dried beef, the ubiquitous jerky, and handed one to Tom, who eyed it with disgust and said, 'Is this the best you got to offer? Christ A'mighty. You put your hand right here, on my stummick, an' that knobbly thing you feel, that's my backbone.'

O'Brien also fetched out two cans of peaches, which he opened with his jack-knife. He passed one across to his prisoner, then sank down onto the warm sand across from him and started fishing the golden, syrupy slices out of the can with his fingers. They were cool—canned peaches were nearly always cool—and melt-in-the-mouth.

'You got a name, mister?' Tom asked after a while, speaking with his mouth full. 'Or do I jus' go on callin' you "mister"?'

'Name's O'Brien.'

Tom had heard of him. 'You killed the Timberlake boys,' he said. 'Down in Fort Smith, 'bout four, five years ago.' He thought about it for a moment, then said, 'Oooh, boy. You're gonna make a fine prize when my buddies catch up with you, O'Brien. You'll suffer for a fortnight before they let you die.'

O'Brien said, 'They've got to catch me first.'

'Oh, they'll do that all right. An' when they do...' He let the sentence hang, figuring to allow O'Brien's imagination to conjure up all manner of gruesome punishments.

When he decided the notion had taken hold in O'Brien's mind, he said, ''Course, it could be that I could help you there.'

'Oh?'

'Sure. You let me go free an' I'll call 'em off.'

'I'm not letting you go, Tom. Best you get that into your skull once and for all.'

Unabashed, Tom went on, 'I meant what I said las' night. About that five thousand dollars. I'm good for it, if that's what's worryin' you.'

'It's not.'

'All right—six thousand.'

'Tom, I'm not interested.'

Tom eyed him keenly, curious now. He

had never yet met a man he couldn't buy. Everyone had a price. It was just a question of finding out what that price was.

'Ten thousand,' he said quietly.

O'Brien finished his peaches and set the empty can aside. 'I thought you wanted to sleep,' he said.

Tom tossed his empty peach-can away and wiped his big, horny palms down his pants'-legs. Again he let loose a noisy, exaggerated yawn. He wanted O'Brien to lower his guard, to assume that he was worn out and no immediate threat. 'All right,' he said. 'Name your price. I'm good for it.'

O'Brien got up and went across to the horses, where he untied his coiled lariat. As he came back over, Tom eyed him suspiciously. 'What you gonna do with that?'

'I'm tired, Tom. I plan to get some sleep. But I'll sleep a whole lot better knowing you won't be getting up to any mischief.'

'Hey, now—!'

O'Brien took hold of him by one

shoulder and pushed him closer to the slim bole of the tree, then, after a brief struggle, set about lashing him to it.

'All this is goin' down on your account, O'Brien,' Tom said through clenched teeth. 'You're gonna pay for every mean-minded little trick you've pulled on me so far, I swear it!'

'Aw, shut up an' go to sleep.'

Tom shifted around some, trying to get comfortable. 'I ain't never done you no harm, have I, O'Brien?' he asked.

'No.'

'This ain't personal, then?'

O'Brien's sigh was irritable. 'What are you trying to get at?'

'Jus' wonderin', is all. If this ain't personal, how come you're so dead-set on takin' me in? It's not for the money. You've already turned down twice what you'd make if you got me to Brigham—'

'*When* I get you to Brigham.'

'Why, then?'

'Tom, you wouldn't understand.'

53

'I'm curious.'

'Well, you know what curiosity can do. Just—'

'I know, I know. Go to sleep. That's if a man *can* go to sleep trussed to a tree, which I doubt.'

O'Brien ignored him, instead scanning the distance. Nothing moved out there, just the cooking air. And despite the damage he had inflicted upon the town, he didn't really expect pursuit from Purgatory. At the moment the desert was his greatest ally, for few men would cross this sun-smashed wilderness if they could help it, no matter how fired-up they might be, if you'll excuse the pun.

But that only made him wonder why *he* had chosen to cross it. The west was full of badmen. He could almost certainly have chosen an easier bounty to collect than this one. But that wouldn't have presented such a challenge. And if there was one thing upon which O'Brien thrived, God help him, it was a challenge. The bounty money was but a secondary consideration, for he had never been a greedy man, and only ever craved a cent more than he could spend.

Again he looked back the way they'd come, brushing aside the buzzing flies attracted to the spot by the remnants of peach-syrup. He was a man of contradictions, a peaceful man in a violent occupation. His father had been a lawman down in Colorado, and from him O'Brien had inherited not only a strong sense of justice and injustice, but also a desire to do something to ensure the one and stamp out the other. But O'Brien's father had been a stubborn, unyielding man who lived by the book. O'Brien himself was no less tenacious, but a whole lot more flexible; his mother had instilled that in him, along with compassion and understanding and a propensity for tenderness.

He closed his eyes. The muggy, unrelieved air did nothing to make him feel less weary. Suddenly it all caught up with him, the tension of the previous evening, the long, hard ride through the night, the uncertainty of the desert-crossing that still lay ahead.

O'Brien slept.

He woke up some time around the tail-end of the afternoon, hot and dry-mouthed, his skin itchy and sore with sweat. But at least the heat of the day was finally sinking down into the earth and the air was turning a little fresher.

He untied his prisoner and fried bacon and beans in a skillet. The food was rough and ready but welcome enough and, in its own way, reviving. Afterwards, they re-tightened their saddles and prepared to move out. Before they did, though, O'Brien took some pegging strings from his saddlebags and told Tom to cross his hands over his saddlehorn.

Tom gave him and the strings a wary look and said, 'What the hell are they for?', to which O'Brien replied, 'You'll find out.' Tom knew what they were for, of course, but had their purpose confirmed as soon as O'Brien tied his hands tight together and anchored them to his saddlehorn.

'Aw, now come *on*, O'Brien—!'

'Shut up,' O'Brien cut in. 'And ride.'

The desert unfolded beneath them, flat

and patchy with brush. As darkness fell in a fine black powder, it came alive with sidewinders and jackrabbits, desert tortoises and Gila monsters, but as near as O'Brien could tell, no other men. He held them to a steady walk, cold now, even with his wolfskin jacket buttoned to the throat.

''Course,' Tom said about an hour later, 'this is a hell of a way to treat a sick man.'

O'Brien said, not believing it, 'You telling me you're sick?'

'Uh-huh,' Tom replied, and his normally-harsh voice quivered a bit. 'Doctor up in Twin Falls said I only got maybe half a year left to run.'

O'Brien glanced over at him with a frown. Ordinarily he would have dismissed such a statement as a desperate lie, but there was something in Tom's voice that made him wonder. 'What's wrong with you?' he asked.

Tom shrugged impatiently. 'Aw, I dis-remember all the details,' he said vaguely. 'You know what kinda fine, speechifyin' words them doctors use. But it's got nine letters in it, an' the doctor said I could die of the first four alone.'

'What's he say you've got?'

Tom looked across at him through sad eyes, and even in the poor light O'Brien could tell he was being absolutely sincere. He swallowed hard and pronounced carefully. 'Ha-li-to-sis.'

O'Brien's frown deepened. 'Halitosis?'

Tom sighed heavily. 'That's what he said.'

'You sure?'

'You think I'd lie about a thing like that?' Tom asked testily.

'Well, if that's what he said, I've got some good news for you. Tom. Halitosis just means you got bad breath.'

'You a medical man now, as well as a bounty hawk?'

O'Brien shrugged. 'Take it or leave it.'

Tom left it, leastways for about another half-mile. Then he looked over at O'Brien's profile and said, after a moment, 'Do it *really* mean I got bad breath?'

O'Brien nodded. 'It do.'

Tom's relief was genuine. 'Well, I'll be damned!' he said as he let out his breath. 'You know, I paid that goddam pill-roller twenty bucks to tell me that! *An'* ten dollars to one of his cronies for a second opinion.'

Instinctively O'Brien shied away from him and wrinkled his nose in distaste. 'Tom,' he said with feeling, 'I could've told you your problem for nothing, believe me.'

They followed more or less the same pattern for the next few days, travelling through the cool nights and resting up from noon till dusk. Tom bitched a lot, as you might expect; about the heat; the cold; that he was hungry; that he was thirsty; that he didn't think a hell of a lot about the food O'Brien was providing for him. But as the days went by, a strange kind of camaraderie developed between them. As the warm afternoons slipped away and they sat beneath what shade they could find and smoked cigarettes or just tried to ease their heat-sore joints, Tom expressed opinions on just about every topic. It didn't matter if he knew what he was talking about or not—he just liked to hear the sound of his own voice.

But in his own way he was likeable enough, if you overlooked his unfortunate tendencies towards homicide and larceny. Orphaned young, he'd joined the army in the hope that he might be able to find a place for him in life. Trouble was, Tom hated taking orders, and rather than waste good money buying his discharge, he'd simply stolen away from his garrison one dark night and never looked back. Hell, he said indignantly, he wasn't the only one. The army was famous for its deserters. And that was certainly true. After that, he'd just kind of fallen in with a bad crowd and, well, O'Brien knew the rest of it.

O'Brien refrained from comment. Maybe Tom *had* fallen in with a bad crowd. Maybe he was just bad from the start. It wasn't O'Brien's job to pass judgement. But it was true enough that circumstances dictated the course a man's life followed. Some folks were lucky and got the breaks. Others weren't, and didn't. Sometimes an unlucky man bit the bullet and tried to make his own luck. Other times it was easier to turn to outlawry. Not every man had enough strength to be honest.

The desert stretched on, unchanging. By day they cooked, by night they froze. But with every mile they put between themselves and Purgatory, O'Brien felt a little easier. He kept an eye on their backtrail, of course, but saw no other signs of life back there in the golden, shimmering distance.

Something back there *was* moving, though, and heading their way.

They reached the sump O'Brien had spoken of and refilled the by-now depleted skins. The pool was a miniature oasis in an otherwise infertile solitude, and Tom was all for staying there awhile. But the sump made O'Brien feel edgy. It was a magnet that would draw people from miles around, if they knew about it, and O'Brien, usually a gregarious enough individual, had no particular desire to meet other folks right now. They might be friends of Tom, or men who would try to take Tom away from him in order to claim the reward for themselves.

So they stopped there for the afternoon alone, and then moved on again after dark.

Mid-morning of the fifth day, the sand and shad scale of the desert began to give way to a great expanse of smooth-edged gravel, and as the morning wore on, so the gravel gave way to cracked, hard-as-iron mud flats encrusted with salt. In the far, far distance O'Brien saw the jagged peaks of the Rockies soaring skyward, purple against blue, and knew with some relief that they were nearing the end of their journey. They came to a spring surrounded by yucca and sagebrush, and not so very long afterwards a trail of sorts began to wind up and through limestone rocks that were all cliff and crag. Meagre woodland sprang up ahead like the stubble on a sleeping giant's chin, and creosote shrub and short, wiry grass stippled the wrinkled terrain to either side of the trail.

O'Brien sat up straighter in the saddle to ease the pressure on his back. He felt tired, for even with Tom tied securely he had not allowed himself to relax completely, and he was itchy with caked salt and he longed for a bath.

'Make the most of it, O'Brien,' Tom said, breaking in on his line of thought. 'Your moment of glory, I mean. Yessir, you ought to be quite a celebrity after this. The man who fetched in Omaha Tom alive.'

O'Brien brushed flies away from his face.

'You know you done broke my little Polly's heart, takin' her man away from her like you did?' Tom continued.

O'Brien shook his head. 'Hearts don't break that easily, Tom.'

'Polly's will. She worshipped me, you know.'

'Well, Polly's the least of your concerns now. And I'm sure she won't lack for consolation.'

'Aw, that's a hell of a thing to say to a feller.'

O'Brien touched the brim of his hat. 'My apologies,' he said gravely. 'I didn't know you were so sensitive.'

Tom flexed his fingers and winced. 'Hey,' he said. 'How 'bout givin' me a break from these here goddam ropes? They're so damn' tight they've stopped the flow.'

O'Brien shook his head. 'Uh-huh. This close to town, you might figure to do something rash.'

'Well, you could hardly blame me. You *do* know they're gonna hang me when they're through tryin' me? Them Mormons at Brigham.'

'You picked it up,' O'Brien reminded him without criticism. 'Now you got to carry it.'

Tom snorted with disgust. 'You're a heartless bastard, you know that?' But almost at once he moderated his tone. 'Look, what if I give you my word? All I'm askin' is for you to untie me. Judas, I'll feel how tight a rope can get soon enough, won't I? I mean, if you're dead-set on takin' me in, at least let me ride in like a man.'

O'Brien shook his head in wonder. 'Just out of interest,' he said. 'Don't you ever get tired of listening to your own voice all the time?'

Tom only said, 'How about it? Huh?'

O'Brien glanced down at his prisoner's hands. They looked chafed and bloodless. Maybe he *had* tied them too tight. His gaze travelled up to Tom's face. Tom wore a look of angelic innocence. O'Brien wondered if he'd meant what he said about riding into town like a man. Could he be trusted to keep his word?

Tom swallowed hard and said, 'Look, I know it probably ain't worth much, my word. But...well, a man gives me the benefit of the doubt, I don't let him down.'

O'Brien held back, still considering, then said, 'Aw, hell...' He reached across with one hand, figuring to untie the ropes quickly, before good common sense took over and he changed his mind, but paused before starting on the knots that bound Tom to his saddlehorn. 'I'm trusting you now, Tom. I mean it. Break your word and so help me, I'll be all over you like a rash.'

Tom looked grateful. 'You got no worries on that score, O'Brien. I swear it.'

O'Brien unfastened the pegging strings and Tom heaved a sigh of relief as they came loose. He massaged his wrists with a look of euphoria on his face.

'Better now?' O'Brien asked irascibly, hating himself for having shown a sign of weakness.

'A whole lot better,' Tom replied. ''Fact, they's only 'bout one other thing that'd make me feel better still. *This!'*

He threw himself sideways out of the saddle and his full weight—about a hundred and ninety pounds—slammed into O'Brien with all the force of an express train. The pair of them together went flying over the far side of O'Brien's mustang and crashed hard into a cluster of sagebrush, all arms, legs and yelling.

At once they began to grapple, hands twisting into claws as each sought to best the other. Hats flew wildly in two directions. Someplace deep in his mind, O'Brien told himself he'd been a stupid, soft-hearted, gullible fool to have trusted such a scheming, lying, no-good, double-crossing, motherless, fatherless bastard the way he had.

Then they went over together in a shower of dirt and snapping sage and O'Brien landed on top.

They wrestled madly. Tom was swearing under his stinking breath, one foul word after another, a whole stream of them. He tried to gouge O'Brien's face but O'Brien strained backwards out of reach. Then Tom thrust one shoulder up off the ground and that pushed O'Brien back further still, so that they both smashed over into their sides.

They rolled some more, each trying to get in a kick or a punch whenever he spotted an opening. Then they came apart and each rolled away from his opponent. There followed a race to see who would regain his feet first. It was a tie. O'Brien went for his gun, but because he had to slip the restraining thong off the hammer before he could draw it, that slowed him down a fraction, which was all the time Tom needed to scoop up a fist-sized rock and swing it at him.

O'Brien saw it coming and tried to dance backwards out of reach. He very nearly made it, but not quite. The blow grazed him on the forehead and he stumbled, momentarily seeing stars, then tripped on some low vegetation and went down with his .38 slipping from leather. Tom yelled something triumphant and went after him, sensing victory. He brought the rock down, intending to turn O'Brien's brain into mincemeat, but O'Brien returned to his senses just in time and rolled to one side. The rock thudded into the ground and dirt exploded from beneath it.

Even as O'Brien was coming back onto his feet, however, he saw Tom snatching his fallen Colt up off the ground. With a snarl that was more animal than anything else, Tom aimed the gun at him and pulled the trigger. O'Brien threw himself to one side as the gun's thunder blocked his ears. He landed in another mound of sage with a snap and a crackle but fortunately no pop. Scratches opened up on his face and hands but they were only minor and did little to distract him.

He came back up into a crouch and Tom shot at him again, and again O'Brien powered sideways into the screening brush. This time he didn't come up again, he just started snaking away from the last place at which Tom had seen him as fast and as fluidly as he could. A third slug chopped through the foliage behind him, then another. Tom yelled, 'Show yourself, O'Brien! Come on now, or I'll kill you for sure!'

Without warning O'Brien froze, breathing hard, listening, hearing nothing.

The silent seconds grew up into a minute. The minute aged rapidly and became two.

'Damn you...' Tom said softly, speaking through teeth clamped tight.

Another quarter of a minute passed.

O'Brien heard a faint rustle of disturbed brush. Raising his head just a fraction, he searched for and found the man who meant him harm. Tom was half-crouched about thirty feet away, the .38 grasped firmly in one big hand, scanning the undergrowth for any sign of movement.

O'Brien kept absolutely still.

At last, losing patience and figuring to flush him out, Tom fired the fifth shot wildly into the brush.

O'Brien came back up onto his feet then, and started racing towards him. Tom spun around to face him, his expression red and furious, and brought the Colt up and pulled the trigger again.

The hammer dropped on the sixth chamber.

The *empty* sixth chamber.

The cry that escaped him was a kind of strangulated moan. With a curse he threw the weapon at O'Brien but O'Brien dodged it and flung himself at his erstwhile prisoner. They went over again, down a slope this time, and it seemed that half the loose and hard-packed dirt and brush went with them in a miniature landslide until the ground flattened out again and they came up hard against a tree that shook as they struck it.

Tom was still swearing, telling O'Brien

70

to lay still while he stomped his face. O'Brien hit him in the belly and got a face full of Tom's halitosis for his pains. He hit Tom again, on the jaw this time, and Tom's head snapped to one side and he staggered a bit, bleeding from the lower lip. O'Brien went after him, determined to finish it fast now, but as he came at Tom with his fists bunched, Tom went backwards, away from him, stumbled on a log, reached down, grabbed it up and came forward again, at a run now, swinging his new-found weapon in a wide arc and roaring like a mountain lion.

For just a moment O'Brien was taken completely by surprise. Tom swung the makeshift club at him and instinctively O'Brien brought his right arm up, hoping to ward off the blow. But even as he did it he realised too late that he'd done another very stupid thing, because this time something *did* go pop—his forearm.

He fell backwards, knowing more pain than he could have imagined, and Tom, sensing that at last he had hurt O'Brien

71

bad, came at him once more, swinging the log for all it was worth.

O'Brien ducked, felt the swish of displaced air as the log described an arc above him, moved back again and felt the tip of the thing skim the front of his chest as Tom brought it back the other way.

He backed up still further. There was hardly any feeling left in his right arm now, save a swelling, throbbing sensation that made him feel sick. He was in no position to defend himself. But he knew he couldn't dodge Tom indefinitely. Sooner or later they were going to have to finish this brawl, and when they did, the winner was going to take all.

It was in that moment that someone let loose an almighty roar of defiance and for the briefest instant O'Brien and Tom locked eyes and each of them thought, *That wasn't me.*

In the next moment O'Brien caught a blur of motion from the corner of his eye; some third party was buying into this affair, coming on at a run and swinging a fallen log of their own.

O'Brien used the opportunity to back up a step further, hugging his right arm close to his chest to ease the pain and hold the broken bone together.

Tom twisted around to face the new-comer, some kind of a question spilling from his lips, but it was lost when the newcomer yelled something none of them properly understood and whacked him around the head.

The log cracked Tom's head sideways and the impact of it snapped the makeshift club in two. Tom dropped to the ground in a heap, crawled around a bit and moaned like a tired baby, then sank slowly into unconsciousness.

Silence settled over the sparse woodland.

O'Brien looked at his saviour, wondering if this wasn't all just wishful thinking, an hallucination brought on by the all-too-real pain in his arm, After a moment he licked his lips and said the first thing that came into his head.

'What...what the hell are *you* doing here...Josephine?'

THREE

The thin, wall-eyed redhead didn't answer him right away. She was looking down at the shapeless bundle of clothes that was formerly Tom Barfoot, until at length she said in a small voice, 'I didn't kill him...did I?'

O'Brien swallowed some more and shook his head. 'I doubt it. But when he wakes up, he'll have the mother of all headaches.'

She looked at Tom for a few moments more, trying to convince herself that he would be all right. Only when she was sure she could detect the rise and fall of his broad back, and hear some of the small, snoring sounds he was making, did she finally turn her attention to O'Brien, and realise that he was hurting, too.

At once concern sharpened her blue eyes and she dropped what was left of her log and hurried over to him. 'What's wrong with your arm?'

He said, 'It's broken.'

There. It was out in the open at last, and it had hurt like hell to say it aloud. His right arm, his gun arm, the principal tool of his violent trade—and it was broken. It left him feeling vulnerable somehow, and because he was not used to feeling vulnerable, he felt restless and edgy as well. If this pathetic little girl/woman from Habgood's hadn't shown up, Omaha Tom would have gotten hold of him sooner or later and turned him into pulp. He'd been lucky this time. But what about next?

The saloon girl made a sound of sympathy in her throat and reached out to put her palms on his broad shoulders and force him down so that he sat with his back against the bole of a tree. 'I better take a look at it,' she said. 'You got a knife? I'll have to cut your sleeve away.'

He reached behind him with his left hand and drew his jack-knife from the back-pocket of his dust-coloured cords. She opened the knife out and then set about cutting the sleeve as gently as she could up the inside seam. As she concentrated on what she was doing, he studied her closely.

Without make-up, she appeared much younger than she had back in Purgatory, though still pitifully thin. There was some colour in her gaunt cheeks, for she had caught the sun during her desert crossing, but her lustrous red hair now hung somewhat limp beneath the old felt hat she had jammed atop her head. The remnants of a dying bruise showed clearly on her right cheek, and his lips thinned down when he saw it. Quietly he said one word, a name.

'Falloway?'

She looked at him, then glanced away. 'Uh-huh.'

So. He'd been right. For reasons of her own, she *had* sought to provide a distraction while he got Tom out of Habgood's, and for her pains Falloway had struck her. O'Brien put his head back against the smooth wood of the tree and took some satisfaction from the knowledge that Falloway would never strike any woman, ever again.

His arm was revealed at last. He looked down at it. It had puffed up a little, and was extensively bruised, but at least the skin wasn't broken. Clinically, he told himself that the two ends must have stayed roughly in place, held there by muscle. That should make the setting and mending easier.

'I'm gonna have to re-set it an' bind it up,' Jo said in a quiet, uncertain voice. 'I'll be as careful as I can, but it's still gonna hurt like sin.'

He nodded. 'There's no help for it.'

'You carryin' anything I can use for a bandage?'

'A spare shirt, in my saddlebag.'

'I seen your horses up the trail a-ways. I'll go fetch 'em.'

He had known the horses wouldn't stray far for stumbling on their trailing reins, and now watched her go after them. She was dressed in a check shirt, and her jeans were cuffed at the ankles and gathered in at the waist by a slim brown leather belt. Worn, very old, creased-leather riding boots completed her outfit.

She came back about ten minutes later, leading O'Brien's horses and her own handsome chestnut stallion. He was surprised that she should own such a fine animal, that she should own any animal at all, but then it came to him that she had likely stolen it in order to get away from Purgatory. Which brought back to mind his original question.

What was she doing here?

He bit down on the pain now returning to his fractured arm. Again he thought about the implications of the injury, what it might mean if the thing didn't heal properly, or if, when it *did* heal, he couldn't regain the speed and dexterity that had saved his life on more than one occasion in the past. He thought back to the blow that had caused the damage, the sudden, sickening snap that followed it. Near as he could tell, the break was clean, not splintery. That was something. But this was going to put him out of action for weeks. It was a daunting prospect for so active a man.

Jo tethered the horses on the far side of the sun-dappled, muggy little glade and rummaged around in his saddlebags until she found his spare shirt. Then she came back over, knelt beside him and set about tearing the shirt into strips.

'You want to tell me what you're doing here now?' he asked.

She busied herself with her work, not wanting to look up at him. 'There's not all that much to tell.'

The pain he was in made his voice sharper than intended. 'You don't say?'

She responded in kind. 'Well, what do you want to know?'

'You deliberately waylaid Falloway, didn't you? So I could get Tom out of Habgood's.'

'Uh-huh.'

'Why?'

She thought about it, then said, 'I don't know. You showed me a little kindness. You don't run into much of that in my line of work. I guess it meant a lot to me.

I wanted to do somethin' kind for you, in return.'

'You don't even know me,' he said.

'I knew you weren't like the other men who ride through Purgatory. I don't know what it was, but... Hell, I guess I've seen enough men in my time to know who's straight and who's not.'

Her tongue poked shyly from the corner of her mouth as she tore his shirt apart. 'Anyway, I hung around, you know, waitin' for you to come back out of Polly's room. But when you did, I could tell right off that somethin' wasn't right. Polly wasn't with you, for one thing. An' you an Tom sure didn't look nor act much like the kind of friends you'd said you were.' She fixed him with a speculative glance and asked bluntly, 'Are you the law?'

'No.'

'Bounty man?'

'At the moment.'

'I figured it was somethin' like that.'

'But you still lent a hand?'

'Sure. I got no love for Omaha Tom, not any of 'em, comes to that. Purgatory...'

Her forehead creased as she thought about what she wanted to say, and a troubled look came into her eyes. 'It's a dead town, mister. There's no rules or questions, no law an' order. You look at it an' you think it's all so free an' easy. But underneath, there's all kinds of black things you don't want to know about. It's the kind of town where nobody ever plans to stay. But you end up there when there's nowhere else to go.'

'And that's what happened to you?'

'Pretty much.'

'But you decided to leave?'

Her narrow shoulders rose and fell and she sighed, trying to shake off her bleak, almost introspective mood so that she could get back to business. 'Well, figure it out for yourself,' she said. 'I don't suppose I'd have been too welcome around Purgatory after what I did to help you. Come to think on it, I don't suppose there was too much left of Purgatory, period, once they put all the fires out.'

One hand rose to touch the fading bruise that still showed blue and purple on her sun-caught face. 'I been thinkin' 'bout gettin' out of town for a while now, anyway,' she said. 'I could take it at first. You know, goin' with the men, seein' the way they behaved when the drink was in 'em. But then it's like...it's like you're on a rockin' horse. It's fun at first, you know, excitin'...but when you've had your fill you want to get off. Only you can't. The horse keeps rockin' faster an' faster, an' it's like you wake up suddenly an' realise that sooner or later you're gonna fall off, an' once you do, all the sinful things you've ever seen are gonna catch up with you.'

Again she fixed him with her penetrating gaze. 'That sound crazy to you?' she asked.

O'Brien shook his head.

She paused, then went on, 'That Falloway, when he hit me that night, I guess he kinda made up my mind for me. While all the men were busy fightin' the fires, I got my gear together, st...uh, took some grub from Habgood's larder an' borrowed the best-lookin' horse I could find in the pen.'

82

At last she finished her work. 'Right,' she said, sucking down a deep breath. 'I'm ready, if you are.'

He said, 'Do you know what to do?'

She shook her head. No, she didn't. Well, neither did he, properly, though he had picked up a few tips over the years about doctoring in an emergency, as most folks did in a land where the nearest doctor might be a hundred miles away.

'It broke about here,' he said, pointing to a spot midway down his forearm. 'You'll have to bind it either side to hold it together, then wrap the whole thing tight and rig me up a sling. Think you can do it?'

She held back from replying at once, then drew in her breath some more and said, 'I can do it. But we got to get the bone into line first, don't we?'

O'Brien looked at her and said quietly, 'I'll get the bone into line.'

Resting his right arm across his lap, he probed as gently as he could with his left thumb until he found the slightest bump under the skin. Once he had it located, he sat very still for a while, preparing to do what had to be done.

He felt the girl watching him, but didn't look up at her. His throat grew tight and he screwed his eyes shut a moment to squeeze the sweat out of them.

Jo said, 'Do you want me to—?'

'No,' he said quickly. Then, a little calmer, 'No, it's okay. I just want to make sure I get it right first time.'

He swallowed, paused a moment longer...

When he did it he tried to do it as quickly as he could, to get it over and done with, but there was no possible way to escape or lessen the pain. As soon as he pushed the bone back into line a thousand stars popped in his head and a mixed gasp and cry spilled through his clenched teeth.

He nearly blacked out. The pain consumed him like fire. But some timeless time later, he realised that she was there beside him, holding him and telling him, *Easy, now...easy...* and there were tears in her eyes.

Slowly his heart stopped pounding and

his breathing calmed down and soon he was shaking a bit, but not much. Wordlessly she took his Durham sack from his shirt pocket and rolled him a cigarette, which she put in his mouth and lit for him. The smoke helped to relax him a little, and after a minute or so he was ready to face the next stage of his ordeal.

'You can bind it now,' he said.

'I'll be as gentle as I can,' she promised gravely.

Working slowly, she set about bandaging his arm, and though she tried to be as good as her word, it still hurt like sin, just as she'd predicted. O'Brien sat there stiffly in tree-shade and tried to tell himself that it didn't hurt at all, the liar, and concentrated not so much on the pain as just not yelling aloud.

A thousand or so years later she finished the job and as the pain subsided to a dull but insistent throb once again, he released his breath and wiped his sweaty face with his left sleeve.

'You all right?' she asked anxiously.

'Uh-huh.'

'I've got some supplies left,' she said. 'I'll make a fire an' fix up some coffee.'

'Use mine,' he said.

'What about him?' she asked, indicating Tom.

O'Brien got to his feet, feeling awkward with the sling tied around his neck. 'Let's take a look.'

They went over to Tom and O'Brien knelt to examine him. He felt nauseous. Tom was sleeping like a baby. One side of his face was swollen and purple where Jo had hit him. O'Brien thumbed back his eyelids and checked his pupils. Once he was satisfied that Tom had sustained no more serious injuries, he told the girl to fetch his pegging strings and tie Tom's arms behind his back.

By now the noon heat was fearsome and O'Brien was starting to feel the effects of the fight and its aftermath. Jo must have seen it in the sluggish way he moved around, and once again took charge, telling him to sit down and rest, that she would handle everything. She did, too; she rustled up coffee and sliced off some suspect-smelling bacon and fried it with some beans in his skillet, and though he said he wasn't hungry, she told him he must keep his strength up, so he ate, and the food was good.

'You didn't mind me ridin' after you, did you, mister?' she asked uncertainly, a few minutes later.

O'Brien glanced up at her. 'Why did you?' he asked by way of reply.

Her response was pitiful in its honesty. 'I guess I got no place else to go.'

He tried to hide his frown. He was beholden to her, that was obvious. And when they got to Brigham, he would make sure she got a share of the reward money. She'd earned it. But there was very little room in his life for excess baggage, and that's what she would be if she expected to tag along with him.

Still...

There was something about her, the fact that she was simple, vulnerable, had been ill-used by cleverer, more devious men, that made him feel protective of her, and it was a feeling that only added to his sense of unease. Not for the first time he cursed his benevolent streak. And yet he couldn't look at her now and not want to do something to make her life a happier one. She was one of those people who'd never had enough luck or opportunity to make something of herself. But maybe with his help there was still a chance to change all that.

'You didn't mind...did you?' she persisted.

'It's lucky for me that you did,' he said. Something occurred to him then and he said, 'My name's O'Brien, by the way. Is your name really Josephine?'

'Uh-huh,' she said, but almost immediately she shook her head instead. 'No. It's Teresa. Teresa Olsen. But Josephine...I don't know, it's just such a pretty name.' She fell silent, embarrassed maybe, picked up a dented old enamel mug and blew steam off the surface of her black, bitter coffee. After a minute or so she asked carefully, 'Is Josephine... Is that your wife's name?'

'I'm not married.'

'So who's Josephine?'

'You ever hear of Napoleon Bonaparte?'

'Sure. He was a Frenchman.'

'Well, Josephine was his...paramour.'

She was impressed.

'Do folks call you Teresa or Terry?' he asked.

'Terry, mostly.'

About twenty feet away, Tom stirred a little and said, 'Aaaahhh...' Five minutes after that he rolled over onto his side, discovered that he was hog-tied again, sat up awkwardly in the dirt and said, 'Hey, what's the big idea—?' He saw the girl then, and scowled. 'What's she—?'

O'Brien set his plate aside and jabbed a finger from his good hand in Tom's direction, which instantly shut him up. 'Before you start shooting off at the mouth again, I got one piece of advice for you, Tom,' he said. 'You only get the one chance. Understand me? From here on in, you'd better walk real soft around me. Keep quiet, and do what I tell you, or the way I'm feeling right now, I'd be just as happy to take you in *across* the saddle as *astride* it.'

Tom's dark eyes shuttled from O'Brien to the girl. He knew who she was, he just couldn't figure out where she'd come from, or what she was doing there. He opened his mouth to say something, then thought better of it and fell silent. A moment later, however, he said, 'Hey, O'Brien. No hard feelin's, huh? I mean, I had to try it, didn't I? Jesus Christ, they' gonna *hang* me in Brigham!'

O'Brien offered him a withering glance. 'I'll tell you something, Tom. I'm thinking about saving them the trouble and doing the job right *here.*'

Tom licked his dried, bloody lips, then spat into the tufty grass. 'I sure could use some o' that coffee,' he said.

'I bet you could.'

'Aw, have a heart! Can't you see I'm hurtin'? I got me a headache you could paint in oils, here!'

O'Brien sighed. He knew that what had happened was as much his fault as anybody's. He should have known better than to trust Tom. But he had trusted him, and now he was paying for it. God, he was paying for it.

'You're not gonna hold this agin me, are you, O'Brien?' Tom asked in a sickly, wheedling tone. 'I thought you an' me...you know...we was friends, after a fashion.'

Relenting again, and annoyed with himself because of it, O'Brien said, 'Aw, for God's sake give him some coffee, Terry.'

The girl eyed him searchingly. 'Are you sure?' she asked. 'After what he did to you...'

'I'm sure,' O'Brien growled impatiently. 'I've got no other way of shutting him up, short of hitting him on the head with another length of wood. At least while he's drinking he won't be whining.'

The food and coffee, coupled with the heat of the day, made O'Brien feel pleasantly drowsy. Nothing would have pleasured him more than to have rested up a while in this peaceful, leafy bosque. But, no more than about twenty miles to the east now, Brigham beckoned. If they left right away, he reckoned they could reach it by suppertime.

Shaking off his fatigue, he got up and went to tend to the horses as best he could with the use of just one hand. The animals were looking ribby and wilted, dust-streaked and a little glazed in the eye. Glancing across their backs as he re-tightened buckles, he saw that Terry looked pretty much the same way, for the desert crossing had likely been harder on her more than anyone, and she'd done well to cross it as she had.

Still, it had taken its toll. As he watched her gather up his cooking gear and carry it across to him, he realised that she was dead on her feet, and that made him consider again whether or not they should stay where they were for the time being, and move on again at first light tomorrow.

It was tempting. But Mormon stronghold though it was, Brigham held its enticements, too. The promise of an all-over bath and sleep enough for a fortnight in a bed as soft as a grandmother's heart. It was a hard combination to refuse. Besides which, he should really get his arm checked by a doctor as soon as he could.

Tom struggled reluctantly to his feet just before they were ready to pull out, complaining that he wouldn't be able to sit a saddle with his arms all strung up behind him like they were, but all his grousing fell on deaf ears. O'Brien took hold of him by the shoulder and pushed him across to his horse. He told Tom to put one foot in the stirrup, then got his left shoulder under Tom's ass and boosted him up and across leather. He and Terry then pulled themselves up into the saddle, and leading Tom's horse behind him, O'Brien led them back up onto the trail. Only once did they stop, to find O'Brien's Colt and retrieve his and Tom's discarded headgear. Then they resumed the final stage of their journey.

O'Brien held them to a steady walk throughout what was left of the afternoon. He didn't want to shake himself around any more than he had to. The town came into sight a little over two hours later, a neat and orderly community that was still expanding in a grid formation along the west bank of the Great Salt Lake, with a Union Pacific station house set a little off to the south and the shining rails of a spur line curving north to south right past it and on through the centre of town. The sun was sinking towards the west as they rode the last half-mile down a shallow grade that fed into the basin where the town had grown up, with sunlight winking amber and gold off the rippled surface of the water behind the buildings in a series of cryptic heliographs.

The day was winding rapidly towards evening, and Main Street was slack with wagon, horseback and pedestrian traffic, but a few of the locals still abroad paused momentarily to follow the progress of the three newcomers as they rode in, and that was hardly surprising, for they were an unusual trio, to say the least: O'Brien, with one bare arm hanging in a sling, Tom, with his arms knotted behind his back, and Terry, drooping slump-shouldered in her stolen saddle, bringing up the rear.

They reined in at the sheriff's office, where O'Brien helped his prisoner to dismount and then escorted him inside and waited while the sheriff, a short, stout man with two wives and hair the colour of barbed wire, satisfied himself that Tom was indeed who O'Brien said he was. Then the lawman took a ring of keys off a peg in the wall and led them into a stone-built cell-block, and when he untied Tom and locked him in one of the cells, Tom at once flexed and rubbed his hands and massaged his arms to restore circulation. For a man who was rapidly approaching a date with the ultimate fate, he didn't appear unduly concerned. In fact, he even had the gall to offer O'Brien a grin.

'No hard feelin's?' he asked through the bars. 'About your arm, I mean?'

O'Brien shook his head in wonder. No matter what you thought of a man who robbed and killed for a living, you had to admire his brass. And there was little to be gained from bearing a grudge against a condemned man. 'Why don't you ask me again in a couple of months' time?' he invited.

Tom said, 'You never know, I might jus' do that,' and he offered a jaunty salute. 'See you aroun', O'Brien.'

O'Brien's voice was sincere when he said, 'Not if I see you first.'

Back in the outer office, the sheriff signed a paper and told O'Brien to take it across to the bank in the morning, where it would be honoured for payment of the full five thousand dollars on Tom's head.

'From the looks of you, I'd say you've earned your money,' the sheriff remarked.

'You're not wrong there,' O'Brien agreed. 'Have you got a doctor around here?'

'Doc Munday,' the sheriff replied. 'Got an office above the hardware store two blocks down the street, on your right. But Doc'll be home by now, enjoying his supper. 'Less it's urgent, I suggest you go see him in the morning.'

It was true enough that O'Brien felt lousier now than ever, but at no time had his injuries been life-threatening. He could wait. 'I'll do that, sheriff,' he said with a nod. 'Thanks.'

He pocketed the bank order, said so-long and rejoined Terry out in the cooling dusk. The girl was dozing in the saddle. He stood a moment on the boardwalk, watching her as she swayed ever-so-slightly back and forth. He tried to compare her to the painted doxy he'd first encountered back at Habgood's, but it was difficult. Away from Purgatory, without all the rice powder and rouge, she looked to be exactly what she had likely been all along; a naive, eager-to-please, child-like, confused young girl. He wondered about her past, how she had come to wind up at Habgood's. But that was none of his affair. What mattered now was that she had broken away from that kind of life. Once she had been resigned to it, but now she was trying to do something to change and improve it.

'Hey,' he said.

Her eyelids fluttered and she came awake with a start. 'Wha...? What? Uh, I...'

'It's all right. Come on, climb down

here.' He reached his billfold out of his back pocket. 'Here. I want you to take some money and go book us a couple of rooms at that hotel across the street. See if they can fix up a couple of good hot baths in our rooms, as well.'

She took the wallet and helped herself to some bills, but looked up at him curiously. 'Two rooms?' she queried.

'Uh-huh.'

'You don't...I mean... We could share. Save you some money. I wouldn't mind, honest.'

'Don't worry about the money,' he said, even though he knew the money had nothing to do with it.

This went deeper, was more basic. He was a man. She was a woman. And they both knew that she was there for the taking. That he had no desire to take her and use her just like every other man she had ever met left her feeling confused and uncertain. Such had been her previous experience that she could not understand that some men actually treated women with respect.

'Where will you be?' she asked after a while.

'I'll be taking our horses down to the livery,' he replied, unbuckling his saddlebags and her carpetbag from their mounts and indicating that she should take them along with her. 'And unless you want to be hanged for a horse-thief, I'll pay the hostler to board your animal till its rightful owner comes to claim it.'

She nodded placidly, content to go along with whatever he said. 'Thanks,' she told him with a dip of the head. 'You been awful good to me, O'Brien.'

He only shrugged uncomfortably. 'Get along, now,' he said. 'And don't forget about those baths.'

With his business at the livery stable concluded, he stopped by the dry goods' store and bought himself a couple of new shirts, then headed for the hotel. Lights were showing at windows now, for evening was finally upon them. He gave the clerk his name, was given a key in return, and climbed the stairs to his room.

Inside, he propped his sheathed Winchester against the wall and put his purchases on the dresser, then got the lantern working and saw by the low, smoky glow a galvanised tub sitting in the middle of the floor with steam rising rapidly off the surface of its liquid contents.

With some relish, he stripped down to all but his make-shift sling and gratefully immersed himself in the water. For the next three-quarters of an hour, his only company was a bar of lye soap and a couple of awkwardly-rolled cigarettes. A bottle of whiskey would have been nice, but save for those isolated little pockets of lawlessness such as Purgatory, Utah was a dry territory. Still, after the harshness of the desert, just the bath alone was a luxury he remained determined to enjoy to the full.

When his skin started to wrinkle, he climbed out of the tub and discovered just how hard it could be for a one-armed man to dry himself off. Though the soak had revitalised him up to a point, however, he knew there would be no substitute for a good night's sleep, so he decided to pass on dinner and crawl straight into bed instead.

Despite his obvious exhaustion and the rigours of that particular day added to all the hardships of the days which had preceded it, despite the comfort of crisp white sheets and a soft feather mattress and big, yielding pillows that moulded themselves to him like oversize marshmallows when he lay his head upon them, his sleep turned out to be fitful and disjointed, mainly because he kept trying to roll onto his right side every time he dozed off.

He rose early the following morning, as was his custom, and soon realised that it was a whole lot easier getting dressed when you had two hands to work with rather than just one. It took him about twice as long as usual to button up one of his newly-purchased shirts and then tuck it into his cords. Neither was hauling on his low-heeled, spurless boots much easier. It was hardly worth buckling on his gunbelt, so instead he took the Colt, now freshly-loaded, and tucked it into his sling, where it would be handy enough for his left hand in the unlikely event that he should need it.

In the corridor, he toyed briefly with the idea of knocking at Terry's door to see if she was awake, but the girl had a way of somehow making him feel as if he had adopted her, and he concluded that it was probably best not to encourage such a notion. Instead he went down into the street, found a cafe and ordered breakfast, and then went in search of the doctor's office.

Dr Jefferson Munday turned out to be a tall, brisk man with a thick, fuzzy beard that was only marginally lighter grey then his thinning, once-wavy hair. He was about fifty years of age, with a brawny build and liquidly blue eyes which surveyed the world from behind frail-looking *pince-nez*. His office was small and cluttered with books and apparatus, and it stank of pipe tobacco, but the doctor himself was affable enough in his rusty black Prince Albert and fancy brocade vest.

'Come in,' he said, taking an old, well-chewed briar from his mouth when O'Brien rapped at his partly-open surgery door. 'How can I help you?'

O'Brien explained who he was and what had happened to him and how Terry had helped to patch him up. Munday nodded all the way through it, then put his pipe into an ashtray, got up from behind his scratched old desk and told him to take off his shirt and go sit up on the cracked-leather examination table over by the pebbled-glass window.

O'Brien did as he was told, withdrawing the .38 from the sling first and setting it to one side. A few moments later, he heard the doctor say, 'Merciful heaven!'

Munday was staring at all the scars that still showed in thin, pale, pinched areas here and there across his chest, arms and shoulders. For the first time, O'Brien felt vaguely self-conscious of them, and cracked a sour grin. He guessed he *had* been around some, and no mistake. A spell as a prize-fighter in his younger days had cauliflowered his ears for him, and looking back, it seemed that he'd been dodging fists, bullets and knife-blades ever since, not always successfully.

Regaining his composure, and refraining from further comment, Munday then went to work unwrapping the strips of shirt that held his arm together, and examined the arm itself with long, sensitive fingers. At length he did some more nodding and said, 'You fractured the radius, but as near as I can tell, the ulna—that's this here bone beneath it—remained intact. It was a clean break, you say?' O'Brien nodded. 'And it's not giving you any sharp or sudden stabbing pains?'

'No.'

'How about that knock on your forehead? No double vision? Headaches?'

'Only what you'd expect.'

The doctor did some more probing. 'Hmmm,' he said. 'You lined the bone up well enough.' He went to a glass-fronted cupboard and took out some bandages, then gently but efficiently re-bound the arm and tied an altogether more presentable-looking sling around his patient's neck. 'You won't be able to use your arm for at least six weeks, I'm afraid,' he said. 'Six weeks minimum. Try to use it any sooner and you may end up back where you started.'

'All right, doc. Thanks.'

'Are you planning to stay in Brigham for a while?'

'I hadn't thought that far ahead.'

'Well, if you're still here in six weeks' time, I'll take another look at it for you. If you've moved on by then, get another doctor to examine it. But don't think you can rush the healing process. Oh, and by the way. There'll be some muscle-wastage when all those bandages come off again, but don't panic, it'll soon come back with some steady, light work. The important thing right now is just to rest it and allow the bone to knit.'

'Thanks, doc. How much do I owe you?'

Munday told him and he paid up.

As Munday pocketed his fee and helped O'Brien back on with his shirt, he said, 'Tell me something, Mr O'Brien.'

'If I can.'

'Don't you ever get tired of the kind of life you lead?' The doctor took off his *pince-nez* and indicated all the scars. 'You don't strike me as a particularly brutal man. In fact, I'd say you were probably more intelligent than most.'

'Thanks.'

'So why do you do it?'

O'Brien had no answer for him, at least no answer that could be encapsulated into just one or two sentences. In the end he said, 'It's just what I do. And I guess I've done it for so long now, I don't think to question it any more.'

'I accept that. I know how easy it is for us to fall into a particular rut or routine, to naturally gravitate towards whatever trade or profession we are best suited to. That's how I became a doctor. I just wonder how long you can go on relying on people like me to keep patching you up, that's all.'

It was something O'Brien had never considered, had never had the need to consider.

106

'How old are you?' Munday asked without warning.

O'Brien glanced down at himself, ostensibly to check that all his buttons were fastened, and said hurriedly, 'Thtyeit.'

'What was that?'

'Thirty eight.'

Munday nodded sagely. 'Well, if you'll forgive my candour, Mr O'Brien, I'd say you're getting a little too old for the kind of life you've been leading. And as you grow older, you slow down. Yesterday someone broke your arm. Tomorrow it might be your neck. And each time you get injured, it's going to take you longer and longer to recover. If ever. Perhaps that's something you should bear in mind.'

O'Brien snorted. He'd been called all kinds of things in his time, but never too old. He contemplated himself. He didn't *feel* old. Or *did* he? No. And anyway, no-one was telling him to go out and buy a rocking chair. The doctor had only said he was getting too old for this kind of life.

Aw, hell. He looked at Munday and

cursed the ability of doctors to plant all manner of foolish ideas into other men's minds, then tucked his gun back into his sling and reached for his hat.

'So long, doc. And thanks for the advice.'

Behind him, Munday said sincerely, 'I hope you'll take it, Mr O'Brien—while you still can.'

FOUR

O'Brien left the doctor's office and stood for a moment on Main. Brigham was starting to bustle now beneath the slowly-warming sun. Women were out marketing or taking their children to school. Canvas-covered wagons were trundling ponderously along either side of the railroad tracks. Horseback riders were angling their mounts around them or tying up at racks or in the public corral while, down at the station house, a train whistle blew shrilly and the train itself released a great gasp of black smoke and glowing cinders into the air, signalling its imminent departure.

O'Brien went back down the street, crossed at the first intersection and entered the bank. The cadaverous, sharply-attired manager knew who he was the minute he closed the door behind him, and his lemony expression told O'Brien all he needed to know about the man's attitude toward bounty hunters. 'Sheriff Hartley warn...uh, told me that you would be calling in, Mr, ah, O'Brien. You have five thousand dollars coming to you, I believe.'

'Uh-huh.' O'Brien handed over the bank order, which the manager scanned perfunctorily.

'I assume you'll want the money in cash?'

O'Brien surprised him by saying no. 'I'll take fifteen hundred in cash. I'd like the balance transferred to my account at the Bank of Cochise County, in Tombstone, Arizona. I've got all the details for you here.'

The bank manager raised one eyebrow. A bounty hunter who worked more like a businessman was something new in his experience. 'Very good, Mr O'Brien. We'll attend to it at once.'

A few minutes later O'Brien stepped back out onto the street five thousand dollars better off, and was just about to head back to the hotel, figuring that Terry would almost certainly be up and about by now, when someone called his name. As he turned around, Doc Munday came hustling along the boardwalk towards him, one hand raised to attract his attention.

When he was near enough, the medic said breathlessly, 'Ah, there you are. I was looking for you.'

O'Brien offered him a lop-sided grin. 'Making sure I can still get around without my walking stick, doc?'

Munday only shrugged that off, and dropped his voice to a lower level. 'Actually, I'd appreciate a word, if you could spare me a moment.'

O'Brien picked up the anxiety behind his tone but decided not to comment on it. 'Sure. You can walk me back down to the hotel, if you like.'

The doctor nodded, and together they began to stroll back along the shaded boardwalk. Munday, wearing a derby atop his unruly mop of hair, stuffed his hands deep into his trouser pockets, too preoccupied to acknowledge the greetings of the townspeople they passed as cordially as perhaps he might under different circumstances. Down at the station house, the train gave out another shrill whistle that rolled like a scream across the flats, and slowly began to pull away from the depot, headed for points north.

'So,' O'Brien said easily. 'What's on your mind, doc?'

Munday inclined his shoulders. 'It's probably something and nothing,' he replied, keeping the dark eyes behind his *pince-nez* on the boardwalk ahead of them. 'It's just that, after you left my office, I got to thinking. And the more I got to thinking, the more it struck me that we might be able to...help each other out.'

'Oh?'

111

'Hmmm. You need to rest that arm of yours for a few weeks, and the job I need doing will enable you to do exactly that, *and* earn a few dollars into the bargain.'

'Sounds reasonable. What's the job?'

Munday considered what he was going to say as the train hauled its string of cars groaning and clanking down the centre of the broad street, hissing jets of steam and wheezing like an asthmatic accordion. Watching him, O'Brien saw that his companion was going to great pains to dismiss his forthcoming request as something of little importance. But he wondered about that.

At last the doctor said, 'I have a brother, John. He's a bit older than me, lives in a little out-of-the-way town down in the Four Corners country, name of Rock View.' Looking up and seeing O'Brien's frown, he said, 'No, I doubt that you've heard of it. To put it bluntly, Rock View's little more than a wide place in the road, about three hundred miles to the south and east of here, just this side of the San Juan

River. John trades horses there. He's just opened up a freight business, too. They don't run to electing mayors down in Rock View, but John's the nearest they've got to a head man.

'Well, what with one thing and another, we don't get to see much of one another these days, but John and I *do* keep in touch by letter. Always have. Only... I haven't heard from John now for about three months and...well, I guess it's kind of stupid, but I'm worried about him.'

'Is there any reason why you *should* be worried about him?'

'Nothing—so far as I know. It's just...just a feeling, I guess.'

O'Brien said, 'Has he got any kin?'

Munday nodded. 'A wife and daughter. And yes—they'd have let me know if anything had happened to him. But I haven't received word from any of them, nor replies to any of the letters I've sent in the last few months.'

'Is there a Western Union office in Rock View?'

'There is, but I'm informed that the

lines are down at the moment. And you know how things are. Rock View's just a small and insignificant town, not at all important. There's no telling how long it'll take to repair them.'

'You haven't fallen out with your brother over anything, I suppose?'

'No.'

'Not even unwittingly?'

'Not even unwittingly.'

'It's not possible that he's too busy to write you the way he used to? What with this new freight business and all?'

Munday's shake of the head was emphatic. 'Not John.'

'Have you got *any* idea why he hasn't written, then?'

'I'm at a complete loss, Mr O'Brien. If anything had happened to John, to any of them, I'd have heard about it by now. But I haven't had a word.'

O'Brien considered the doctor's predicament as they came to a halt before the hotel. 'So you'd like someone to go down there and take a look around on your behalf,' he said.

'There's probably some completely mundane, rational explanation for it,' Munday replied. 'And I'd go find it out for myself if I could. But it's not always easy for a man with my commitments to leave town for any length of time. That's what made me think of you. I'd be happy to pay you for your trouble, of course.'

With his newly-acquired cash still stuffing out his billfold, O'Brien was expansive. 'All I'd want is expenses, doc.'

'Oh, but I—'

'I mean it. I didn't have anything better planned, and, well, it's something to do while I'm laid up.'

Munday's relief was obvious. He reached out his right hand, changed his mind and extended his left instead, and they shook. 'I'm obliged to you, Mr O'Brien. I knew I wasn't far wrong in my assessment of you. Stop by my office at, say, midday and I'll have everything ready for you, including a letter of introduction to my brother.'

'I'll do that.'

O'Brien watched the doctor trot off back towards his office and thought about the chore he had just undertaken. It was, as Munday had already said, probably something and nothing. But he didn't have anything better lined up, and even if he had, he could hardly ply his usual trade with a broken arm. This simple task should not only occupy him for a while, but also make for a welcome change of pace.

But almost immediately his face clouded as he remembered Terry. It annoyed him that he should wonder how she would take the news that he'd be leaving town again so soon. They meant nothing to each other. They *didn't*. So why did he feel that they *did?*

He went into the hotel and directly upstairs to her room, where he paused a moment, then rapped at the door. It swung open almost at once, as if she had been waiting there for him just the other side of the portal, and when she saw him, her long, lean face fairly lit up.

'O'Brien!' she said, stepping aside so that he could enter. 'Where you been? I looked in on you about half an hour ago, but your room was empty. I thought...'

She bit off abruptly and her smile turned rueful. 'Aw, never mind what I thought.'

She was wearing what was probably the quietest and most sober dress she owned, a pink affair edged with white lace, cut low at the front, tight at the waist and full and flowing from the hips on down. Some of the tiredness had gone out of her face and she had washed and curled her red hair. She had thought to apply make-up, too, but it had been administered with more subtlety than the customers back at Habgood's probably would have appreciated, and she looked good, though still painfully thin.

He glanced around her room. It was a carbon copy of his own. Sunlight and street-sounds came in through the slightly-opened window. He took his hat off and threw it down onto the chair beside the bed, then turned to face her and raised his right arm a little. 'I thought I'd get the local sawbones to take a look at this,' he explained.

'What'd he say?'

'Providing I rest it for about six weeks,

it should mend good as new.'

'Well,' she said with a smile, 'you won't have to raise a finger while I'm around to help out.'

He squirmed a little at that, and to change the subject, quickly took out the money he'd collected at the bank and offered it to her. 'Here,' he said. 'This is for you.'

Her blue, uneven eyes widened when she saw the stack of bills. 'It's part of the reward I collected on Omaha Tom,' he said. 'I figured you earned this much, at least.'

She looked at him, her expression very hard to define. When she spoke, her voice was quiet. 'I didn't do it for the money.'

'I never said you did. But I'm beholden to you, and I wanted to settle accounts before...'

She regarded him closely. 'Before what?'

'I'm leaving this afternoon. I've got another job.'

She frowned. 'Leavin' town? But... What about your arm? I mean, didn't the doctor say—'

118

'It was the *doctor* who gave me the job.'

She turned toward the window, thinking about what he had said, *really* said, then thought some more. Finally she cleared her throat. 'Can I come with you?' she asked bluntly. 'You mind?'

'I'd as soon you didn't,' he replied, keeping his tone as moderate and reasonable as he could.

'Why?' she asked, turning back to him. 'I've got three hundred miles to cover, and I'm not sure yet what I'll find waiting for me at the end of it.'

'I don't mind that,' she said, a little pleadingly. 'I won't slow you down, I promise. An' I could be real good for you, O'Brien. I could help you a lot.'

Very deliberately, because it was the only kind of language she understood, he said, 'No.'

The silence thickened and clotted, until she reached out and flipped the edge of the bills he still held out to her. 'So what's this for?' she asked, curling her lip in disdain. 'A pay-off to ease your conscience? Christ,

I thought you was different, but you're just like all the rest. You think money can buy anyone.'

There was no point in arguing about it. With a shrug he threw the money down onto the mattress, where it fanned out like a hand of cards, and grabbed his hat. 'So long, Terry.'

'Wait,' she said. The smile she offered him was twitchy and erratic, more like a grimace than anything else. 'Don't let's part this way. I'm sorry. I don't mean half of what I say, it's jus'...' Her fingers knitted together desperately. 'I thought I could stay with you, at least for a while. I mean...how long do you think a girl like me could last in a town like this? An' it's too damn' close to Purgatory for my likin'.'

'You've got money there on the bed and a railroad depot just outside of town. You can go any place you like.'

'Where?' she asked petulantly.

'Haven't you got any folks?'

She snorted. 'Folks!' She spat the word more than said it. 'I'll tell you somethin' about my folks, shall I? My pappy caught me washin' down one mornin' when I was just turned sixteen. He didn't say nothin' right then, but that night he came into my room an'...well, you can guess the rest. That's how I lost my virtue—sixteen years old, to my own pappy!

'I kept that bottled up inside me for near half a year, with him comin' to me whenever he had the chance, an' me too frightened to tell anybody about it. An' you know what my ma did when she found out about it? She beat me! *Me!* Said as how I was a Jezebel who'd led him on!

'Oh, she knew the truth of it, a'course. She'd've had to be blind not to. But I guess it was easier for her to blame me than blame pappy. So I ran away from home, an' I been runnin' ever since. Trouble is, I ain't never had no place to run *to*. That's how come I wound up in Purgatory.'

Angrily she knuckled the tears from her eyes, too mad to give in to them. He stood silent and impassive, watching her. He felt sorry for her. Of course he did. But hers

121

was just one more hard luck story in a land where almost everyone had a hard luck story to tell.

He'd wanted to help her. She needed it. She hadn't struck him as the kind of girl who could get very far without support and encouragement. But there was a limit. The money could help to set her up someplace else. The rest of her problems were none of his affair. He had shown her no more consideration than he'd have shown any other complete stranger down on their luck. He hadn't asked to be saddled with her, and there was no reason on earth why he should be.

But...

Dammit, there was always a *but*.

It wasn't going too far to say that she had saved his life. Had it not been for her intervention, Omaha Tom would have broken a whole lot more than just his arm. Whether he liked it or not, he *was* beholden to her. And she *did* have a point when she said that Brigham was too close to Purgatory for comfort.

'Tell you what,' he said brusquely. 'I'm

heading south-east. If you think you could start life afresh somewhere down there, you're welcome to travel part of the way with me, if you've a mind to.'

Again her whole face lit up and she crossed the room towards him, threw her arms around his neck and kissed him wetly on the cheek before he could do anything about it. 'O'Brien, you won't be sorry, I swear it!' she said. 'You'll wonder how you ever could've gotten along without me, you'll see!'

Some time later, O'Brien went down to Doc Munday's surgery and collected a hundred dollars in expense money and a letter of introduction addressed to the doctor's brother. O'Brien and the medic shook hands once again, and then O'Brien took a slow amble down to the railroad depot, where he purchased two tickets for the next train south, plus passage for his mustang in the horse-car. The train, he was told, was due in at three and would pull out again twenty minutes later. In the event, it puffed and shushed into Brigham at four o'clock and left again at ten after.

O'Brien and his not-altogether unwelcome companion trended south by way of a spur line that kept them on the move for the next day and a half. Terry was good company as they roared across the largely waterless, rocky terrain to the regular *calang-calang, calang-calang* of the cramped, juddering carriage. Once she got started, she was a non-stop talker, which was all right up to a point, but inevitably there came a time when all a man with a broken wing wanted to do was sleep and just get to where he was going. But O'Brien bore it all with his customary patience, telling himself that it couldn't last forever, and that eventually even Terry must run out of topics to discuss.

She had her uses, though. When they stopped once at a Harvey House and O'Brien ordered a steak he couldn't possibly hope to cut into with just his left hand, she was there like a shot, slicing the meat up for him, much to his embarrassment. And when he had an itch in his left shoulder that he couldn't scratch, she told him to stop fidgetting in his seat while she scratched it for him.

He liked her. She was too simple to be anything but honest, and if there was one thing O'Brien admired about all else, it was honesty. But as they powered further and further towards his destination, he wondered when she would decide that she herself had come far enough.

When they reached a little town called Patten, which was as far as the railroad could take them, it seemed to be the best opportunity he was going to get to ask her. She tried to avoid answering right away. Then, when he pressed her on it, she muttered something about maybe being able to go a little further south and east, with him.

Scowling, he said, 'You're planning to stick to me all the way to Rock View, aren't you?'

She batted her eyelashes at him. 'If you'll have me.'

'And that's what you figured to do all along, wasn't it?'

'Well...I kinda hoped. I mean, I got no—'

'I know, I know. You got nowhere else to go.'

'Aw, be fair now,' she said. 'I ain't been no trouble to you, have I?'

Grudgingly he said, 'No.'

She grinned up at him and squeezed his left arm. 'You're a good man, O'Brien. There's not many who'd put up with me like you do.'

O'Brien's sigh was fatalistic. He didn't really feel he had much choice in the matter.

Patten was situated on the north bank of the Colorado River, about eighty miles west of the border with his home state, and about as far again from Rock View. He wondered if the two towns were linked by a stage line. They weren't. They would have to complete the journey on horseback, then.

They went down to the town's only livery stable and Terry picked out a pocket-sized pinto pony of which O'Brien, like all rangemen, heartily disapproved because he perceived its mix of colours to denote weakness. The stable-owner asked seventy dollars for the horse. O'Brien got him down to fifty, and the stable-owner threw in a poor but still-serviceable saddle and bridle as well. They then bought some supplies, paid the local ferryman to haul them across the river and left the town behind them later that same afternoon.

The land was all deep canyons and rounded hills and weird, multicoloured walls of rock. The weather was dry and humid and in no way ideal for such an arduous trek. Mountains angled towards the sky. Occasionally there was graze, but it was scarce. Mostly the country was just rock and dust, an immensity of isolation.

By O'Brien's estimate, they should reach Rock View in three, maybe four days. Only now did Terry finally think to ask him the nature of his job there. There was no harm in telling her about it, so he did.

But the closer they came to their destination, the more seriously he began to wonder what he would find there. There could be any number of reasons why Doc Munday's brother hadn't written to him, of course. Perhaps he'd been involved in an accident. Perhaps he *had* written, but his letters had been lost in the mail. But these reasons could not explain the total and continued lack of contact Doc Munday found so worrying.

Terry bore all the riding without complaint, but as they made camp each night he could tell by the stiffness of her movements that her legs, back and rump were paying the price of horseback travel. They continued on without seeing a soul. But when they made camp two nights later, O'Brien knew they would reach their destination some time the following day.

They camped that night alongside a thin creek, with frogs hopping and croaking in among the reeds and grasses lining the track-littered banks and mosquitoes zipping back and forth across the water's oily surface. O'Brien caught and cleaned out some fish, and Terry built a fire and cooked them.

Using his saddle for a backrest, he rolled and lit a smoke and watched her as she worked. She was the happiest he had seen her so far. She was looking better in herself, too, with every passing day. Her face and body were starting to fill out and she was gradually losing that mean, underfed look. Clean, fresh air, sunshine and decent food were working wonders on her.

He listened to the peace of the evening. The smell of cooking was good in his nostrils. He thought about what the doctor had told him that day back in his office. Maybe he was slowing down. It was nothing to be ashamed of. But his open, rugged life was the only one he knew.

Briefly, and not all that long before, he had considered settling down with a woman. But she hadn't really been for him, and he most certainly had not been for her. And, if he was going to be honest about it, he didn't really see himself as the settling kind. The best he could manage were a few quiet times like this.

Terry slid the fish onto plates and brought them over, and they sat together and ate in silence. Afterwards she poured coffee and they sat in companionable silence. Off in a thicket twenty feet away, the horses stamped or blew air through their nostrils. Some time later, when the night had gathered about them, she moved a little closer so that she could rest herself up against him, and almost before he knew it, he had put his left arm around her and they were quite content just to doze there.

Then—

Without warning O'Brien suddenly tensed. In the distance they heard the single, echoing detonation of a handgun, swiftly followed by a flurry of answering shots. O'Brien pushed himself up onto his feet as Terry, uneasy now, asked him what he thought they meant.

O'Brien shook his head. He didn't know. *Yet.* But it couldn't be anything good. The redhead came up beside him, and they listened for further sounds but heard none. After a moment Terry shivered and bent to poke some life back into the fire, but O'Brien said, 'Leave it.' If there were men out in the darkness using guns, it might be just as well if they didn't advertise their presence any more than they had to.

He reached into his sling and ran his fingertips thoughtfully across the butt of his .38. It was hard to gauge how near, or far, those shots had been. He thought he caught a sound on the faint night breeze. Clattering hooves. He listened for a while longer, but there was nothing else, only fish breaking the surface of the nearby water with little liquidy popping sounds, the croaking frogs, the sound of birds shifting around in tree branches and the occasional passing flutter of bats or an owl.

O'Brien wondered what he should read into the fusillade, if anything, whether or not it was connected in any way with Rock View. A while later Terry offered him a refill for his cup and he allowed himself to relax a notch. There would be time enough to get some answers tomorrow.

But then he froze, and he knew by the way Terry sucked in her breath beside him that she had felt it too, the tremble that ran through the ground beneath them, the drum and throb of many horses being pushed hard, and coming their way.

FIVE

'O'Brien—?'

O'Brien cut the redhead short with one single, important question. 'Have you ever fired a long gun before?'

Terry opened and closed her mouth a couple of times, then shook her head. She was scared. And maybe with good reason. He gestured towards his gear and said, 'Better fetch my Winchester, then.'

'You think we're gonna have to sh-shoot it out with whoever's out there?' she asked, awed by the prospect.

'I doubt it. But it won't do us any harm to be prepared.'

By now they could hear the pulsing throb of approaching horses more clearly as it vibrated through the cool darkness. O'Brien swallowed softly, cursing his broken arm, the feeling of helplessness it gave him, the uncomfortable and hitherto-alien sensation

132

of being at someone else's mercy.

The dying fire threw the weakest of orange glows around the thicket. The animals, sensing the impending arrival of more horses, stamped expectantly and tugged at their picket pins in order to get a better look. Abruptly the croaking frogs and singing crickets in the reeds fell ominously silent, alerted by the presence of newcomers.

Terry came back with O'Brien's Winchester, handling the thing awkwardly, as if it weighed a ton. 'You've got to work the lever to put a shell under the hammer,' he instructed her urgently. She did as he said, all fingers and thumbs in her haste, and obviously unaccustomed to the task. 'Attagirl,' he said when as last she managed it. 'Now, remember. Leave all the talking to me. And don't even *think* about squeezing that trigger unless I start shooting first. Then throw yourself down behind that deadfall yonder and keep yourself flat to the ground.'

She might have replied, but by then the first of the horsemen was coming out of the darkness towards them, having slowed his mount to a cautious walk whilst still out in the darkness.

O'Brien squinted through the poor light in an effort to see him more clearly. He appeared to be a tall but undernourished man in a suit of rusty black broadcloth, a boiled white shirt and a black string tie. Thick, downy white hair fell from beneath his black hat to blend perfectly into an equally-thick beard. His eyes were slits couched in folds of weathered, ruddy flesh, his nose a hooked beak, his mouth apparently lipless, his teeth very square, strong-looking but discoloured. O'Brien put his age at perhaps sixty. He held a carbine across his lap, the fingers of his gnarled right hand curled through the guard and around the trigger and stock.

The rest of his men came out of the shadows just then, having also slowed their mounts to a more sensible pace. O'Brien watched them fan out behind him, and ran his eyes swiftly across them in an attempt to gauge which of them he should keep a closest watch on. They were all of a type—big, brawny, hard-faced bully-boys, firebrands certainly, but not men of the range, as their barely adequate horsemanship ably demonstrated. To a man they carried carbines. No sidearms that he could see. An odd bunch then, for sure.

Then he came to the men just behind the lead rider and drew in his breath, believing for a moment that his eyes must be deceiving him and that he was seeing double in the poor light. But then he exhaled slowly through slightly-parted lips. No, he wasn't going mad; these two were twins.

Each of them had a tall, rangy build. One of them dressed like a banker, in a black Prince Albert over smart grey pants and a chalk-white shirt under a fancy brocade vest. His brother dressed more to O'Brien's own taste, range-fashion, with a plain cotton shirt beneath a buttoned canvas jacket and stiff new jeans beneath a pair of shotgun chaps. Both of them wore smooth-handled guns at their hips, the banker a .38, the cowboy a .44.

They were scrutinising him just as thoroughly as he was scrutinising them. Each of them had a round, clean-shaven, surprisingly pale countenance and dark brown, near-black eyes. Each had the same small button nose and slight, sour twist to his lips. They were in their middle- to late-twenties, as near as he could judge, and beneath their hats—a grey muley and a tan-coloured J.B. respectively—they each wore their black hair short and oiled.

At last the lead rider spoke. 'Well,' he said in a low, measured tone. 'This *is* a homely little picture, isn't it?'

O'Brien nodded. 'It *was*,' he agreed. 'Until you fellers started all that shooting.'

The bearded man nodded to show that the point was taken. 'I apologise if we disturbed you. That wasn't our intent. But we're looking for someone. A single rider, headed this way, we think. You seen or heard anyone pass this way?'

'No-one. Who is it you're after?'

The bearded man, having wrapped his reins around his saddlehorn, now reached his left hand up to scratch at his beard.

He was thin and confident, quietly spoken but obviously used to being obeyed. He ignored O'Brien's question, a fact which was not lost on O'Brien, and asked, 'Who might you be? What are you doing way out here?'

O'Brien paused before answering. Something cautioned him against being *too* honest, and following his instincts, he kept his response vague. 'Oh, we're just passing through.'

'Where are you headed?'

'Mexican Hat.'

The bearded man studied him for a long beat, as if trying to decide whether or not he meant what he said. One of the twins, the banker, heeled his horse forward a couple of steps and said, 'You *sure* you haven't seen a rider pass by this way?'

'I said so, didn't I?'

The other twin piped in, then. 'Mind if we take a look around?' he asked. 'To be sure?'

O'Brien nodded. 'As a matter of fact,' he replied coolly, 'I *do*. My word's always been good enough for folks in the past.'

'Maybe,' said the banker. 'But this is official business. And we don't know *you* from Adam.'

O'Brien said, 'You the law, or something?'

The banker's twin said smugly, 'Or somethin'.'

'Well, unless you're the law, you're just going to have to take my word for it, cowboy.'

The cowboy said, 'Have a care, mister. I can be a bad man to cross.'

O'Brien said, 'That makes two of us.'

The cowboy made a little growling sound in his throat and he started to kick his horse closer, but the bearded man stopped him with one upraised palm. 'No need to turn this into a set-to, mister,' he said. 'Your word's as good as any, I daresay. Could even be better than most, for all we know.' But his slitty little eyes were scanning the campsite, searching, probing, making his inspection as sharp and thorough as he could. 'What did you do to your arm?'

O'Brien made his reply sound casual. After all, there was no point in letting them know the full extent of his temporary disability. 'Aw, just strained it, is all.'

'Well, you'll find Mexican Hat some thirty miles further south, just the other side of the San Juan. You should reach it, no trouble, by tomorrow afternoon.'

O'Brien nodded again. 'Obliged,' he said, adding as if it were an afterthought, 'Say, is there anywhere closer than Mexican Hat where a man can buy some extra supplies?'

''Fraid not. There's nothing in these parts save rocks and dust.'

'I heard there was a town not far from here. Place called Rock View.'

'You heard wrong, mister. My advice is for you to keep riding south.' Advice? The bearded man made it sound more like an order. He touched the brim of his hat to Terry, then unwound his reins. 'Sorry to have troubled you,' he said again.

'No trouble, I guess. Hope you find whoever it is you're after,' O'Brien replied, not meaning a damn' word of it.

The riders turned their mounts away, all but the cowboy twin, who hung back a moment, glaring daggers at him. 'You take good care of that arm, mister,' he said in an undertone. 'And watch your damned lip in future.'

O'Brien grinned tightly. 'Or?' he enquired.

The cowboy said, 'You'd look awful stupid with *both* your arms in wraps.'

O'Brien shrugged. 'No worse than you'd look with your head on back to front,' he replied sociably.

Again the cowboy twin stiffened in the saddle and made to heel his horse in closer, but this time the bearded man called, 'Gene!' and reluctantly the cowboy yanked his horse away and cantered off to catch up with the others.

They disappeared into the darkness. Only when they could no longer be heard did O'Brien release his breath and take his left hand away from the revolver concealed in his sling.

Terry said, in a hushed, confused voice, 'O'Brien! What do you suppose *that* was all about? Who *were* those men?'

He shook his head, his expression grim.

Who were they indeed? And why had they lied about the existence of Rock View? He began to wonder if he hadn't come upon something far more serious than just one brother failing to write to another. 'I don't know, Terry,' he replied after a moment, feeling troubled and suspicious. 'But I'll tell you this much—I sure aim to find out.'

He stood there a moment longer; then, reaching a decision, he kicked dirt onto what remained of the fire. 'Get your gear together, girl,' he said. 'We're pulling out.'

She froze in the act of resting his Winchester up against the deadfall. *'Now? I mean, tonight?* I thought—'

'Something tells me we'd do well to keep our arrival in Rock View as quiet as possible.'

In the darkness she said, scaredly, 'There's more to this business than you thought, isn't there?'

'I reckon.' He looked at her silhouette as she gathered up their cups and plates and went to rinse them in the creek. He didn't want to involve her in this. It was nothing to do with her. Briefly he considered escorting her to Mexican Hat and then coming back on his own. But his curiosity was up. Something strange had happened, or was still happening, out here. He wanted to find out exactly what, and as soon as possible.

They moved out within the quarter-hour.

The night was black and chilly. They followed the course of the creek as it flowed further east, then crossed it and left it behind them about a mile on down the trail, and continued towards the southeast. O'Brien thought about the bearded man, the twins, the rest of the hardcases who rode with them. All he had at the moment was supposition and conjecture. He knew nothing for sure.

The land grew hilly. It was, as the bearded man had said, all rock and dust. Beside him, Terry dozed in her saddle. Then, along towards dawn, they topped a rise and reined in abruptly.

They sat their mounts, looking at the

fallen telegraph pole that measured its length across the trail before them, for a long, heavy moment. O'Brien swung down and went to inspect it closer, already knowing what he would find.

The wires had been cut deliberately. And the pole itself had been felled not by some calamitous act of nature, but rather by a man or men, wielding axes.

Someone had deliberately chosen to isolate Rock View from the rest of the world.

'What does it all mean, O'Brien?' Terry asked anxiously as he climbed back aboard his mustang.

He said, 'I don't know.' He felt tired. His head ached and his eyes felt dull and vacant. He needed sleep just as much as she did.

They rode on, past the fallen pole, deeper into the hill country until the dips and swells had gobbled them up. The horizon took on the faintest strip of silver at its base. Slowly at first, but then with greater speed, light grew and flourished to chase away the darkness. A mile further on, and then they came to another ridge, and directly below them they saw Rock View, huddled against the base of a steep, seamed mountain about half a mile beyond.

They descended the slope and crossed the rock- and brush-strewn basin towards the grey-lit buildings. As they drew nearer, O'Brien took in more details.

He could certainly see why the town had been named. It was dwarfed and dominated by the mountain against which it had been built. At the farthest end of the single street, a cemetery rose up and across the sloping hillside, tiny grey headstones scattered one after another like milestones pointing the way towards eternity. At the base of the hill, the street extended towards them in an arrow-straight line, flanked mostly by frame buildings of varying shapes and sizes.

O'Brien slowed his mustang to a more wary pace and automatically Terry followed suit. The town, he saw, wasn't really all that much bigger than Purgatory, and it seemed to have just one of everything. As they rode closer, they could make out individual signs; a mercantile, a hardware store, a restaurant, a barbershop, a church built close to the cemetery, a stable and public corral, a small hotel and a cluster of residential dwellings.

In virtually every respect it was a town like any other, albeit smaller than most. But something was seriously wrong with the scene before them, and by mutual consent they both reined in at the town limits to study it further.

It was a little after dawn now. The town should be stirring. But the street was empty. There was no traffic, stalled or moving. No pedestrians. A dry breeze blew dust along the street, nudging a tumbleweed along ahead of it, but apart from that, there was no sign of habitation.

O'Brien felt Terry's eyes on him. He turned to face her. He saw the question in her eyes. He said, 'Maybe we'd better take a look around.'

They clucked their horses to a walk and entered the seemingly deserted town, O'Brien panning from left to right ahead of them, searching for any sign of life but finding none. The only sound was the *clop-clop, clop-clop* of their horses' hoofs against the hardpack, the occasional squeak of a loose door swinging on a juiceless hinge.

Another tumbleweed rolled past. O'Brien turned his horse around it. Terry's pinto tossed its head, unnerved by the complete silence of the place. O'Brien ran his eyes along the left side of the street, but only blank, dusty windows returned his puzzled stare. And yet...

And yet...

And yet he couldn't help feeling that they were being watched.

At the end of the street they reined in before the livery stable. Although it had an air of abandonment about it, it looked to be in decent enough repair. But that went for the entire town. A shingle hanging over the open double doors swung lazily in the breeze. It said, MUNDAY'S. Parked down beside the building were two large, heavy-timbered freight wagons. They had obviously been there for some time.

O'Brien pursed his lips. What did this

all add up to? He was damned if he knew. He was just about to turn to Terry and ask if she had any bright ideas, when suddenly, from someplace deep inside the stable, a couple of horses whickered and snorted.

O'Brien and the girl exchanged a look. What were horses doing here if this place really *was* deserted?

The simple answer was that it *wasn't* deserted.

Almost as soon as he thought it, someone behind O'Brien cocked a rifle and said, 'Hold it, the pair of you! Not a move, now, or I'll shoot!'

Terry gave a little gasp but O'Brien only twisted his reins around his saddlehorn and raised his left hand shoulder-high. He turned his head a little, the better to converse with the man who had got the drop on them, but whoever he was, he said, 'Not so much as a twitch, or I'll shoot!'

O'Brien checked the movement, because he sounded like he meant it. The voice was male, aged, scared and angry and desperate all in one, which made for a hell of a dangerous mixture. He sounded like a man just about to run out of string. 'Mr Munday?' he asked carefully.

Silence. He thought for a moment that the rifleman might have disappeared. But then the man said, 'I'm Munday. Who're you? And what's your business here? By all that's holy, I've already told Haven to leave us alone!'

O'Brien's brows met in a frown. He said, 'Who's Haven?'

'Who's H—? Look, whoever you are, just turn around and get out of here! We don't want any more trouble, but by God we've had enough of you people and we're just about ready to start fighting back!'

'Your brother sent me, Mr Munday.'

'That's a lie!'

'He gave me a letter of introduction. Can I reach into my saddlebag to get it?'

'No,' the man behind them replied quickly. Then, his voice calming down a bit, he said, 'We'll do that. Eben—go take a look. And don't you dare try anything, mister. I've got you covered all the while!'

O'Brien and Terry sat still and back-straight aboard their fidgety horses, uncomfortably aware of the long gun trained upon them. From the corner of his vision, O'Brien saw a shadow fall across the dirt to one side of him. He sensed, then heard, a second man—Eben—shuffle up beside him, and listened patiently while Eben unbuckled his saddlebags and delved around inside. Around them the sun climbed higher. Occasional flies, stirring now that the day was warming up, zipped through the air. Beside him, Terry whispered O'Brien's name, and he nodded slowly and said, 'It's all right.'

'No talking, there!'

At last Eben found the envelope, inspected it and said, 'It's got your name on it, John.'

Munday said, 'That doesn't prove anything. Bring it here, let me see it.'

Eben's shadow bobbed back out of sight. O'Brien put mental images to the sounds behind them—Munday passing his rifle across to the other man, taking the envelope in return, tearing it open, unfolding the letter inside, then silence, as he read it.

'What's your name?' Munday asked after a while.

O'Brien told him.

'You know my brother?'

'I broke my arm about a week ago. Your brother took a look at it for me, to make sure we'd set it right.'

'What does my brother look like?'

'What the hell kind of question is that?'

'This note's from my brother, all right. I'd know his fist anywhere. But who're you? Maybe Haven got to this fellow O'Brien before O'Brien could get here. Maybe you're one of Haven's men, *masquerading* as O'Brien.'

O'Brien sighed. It was a fair enough point, he guessed. 'All right,' he said wearily. He described Doc Munday as thoroughly as he could, from the colour of his beard to his distinctive *pince-nez*.

Munday digested that, but still stubbornly cautious, he added one further question. 'Jeff still stinking his surgery out with them foul little cheroots of his?'

O'Brien couldn't resist a smile. 'Last time I saw him, Mr Munday,' he said, 'he favoured a pipe.'

He felt some of the tension dissipate then, and Munday, finally satisfied, said, 'All right. Put your hands down, the pair of you. You've convinced me.' He told them to dismount, then turned around and raised his voice. 'It's all right,' he called out. 'They're friends!'

O'Brien and the redhead swung down and turned to face the doctor's brother. He, like the doctor, was big and sturdy-looking, somewhere in his mid-forties, with hazel eyes and a big moustache and skin that had been cured by the elements. He was dressed in a wash-faded red shirt and brown linsey-woolsey pants, a man used to hard, manual work, but not unintelligent. Sand-coloured hair topped his head, thick but turning prematurely to snow. He brushed his fringe back away from his eyes and offered O'Brien his hand. Almost at once the fringe fell back across his forehead.

O'Brien shook with him and then introduced Terry while, up on the board-walk, the people of Rock View stood in a silent, unmoving line, regarding them inscrutably. There were perhaps fifty of them, men and women but no children, and no-one there was under Munday's forty five, though there were plenty well past Eben's sixty-plus.

'I knew help would get here sooner or later,' Munday said, and O'Brien returned his attention to the brawny horse trader. 'But...' Emotion squeezed his voice then, and he had to swallow and shake his head a bit before it would come back. 'I... You'll have to excuse me. It's just that we...we've been under such a strain here. I'd kind of given up all hope of ever seeing anyone from the outside world ever again.'

A new thought occurred to him then, and he asked intently, 'How on earth did you get past Haven's men?'

O'Brien gave him a questioning glance, and Munday made a sweeping gesture with the hand holding his brother's letter of introduction. 'Haven's got this place locked up tight as a bank vault,' he explained. 'He's got men strung out right the way round the town. We've as good as been under siege here these past months.'

'We didn't run into anyone.'

'No-one at all?'

'Only those men last night,' said Terry.

Munday's interest sharpened still further and he turned edgy. 'What men? Tall, thin fellow with a white beard?'

'That's him.'

'That was Haven. What happened?'

O'Brien told him, watching as Munday's manner grew increasingly agitated. 'They were hunting someone,' he said when he came to the end of it. 'Someone from here?'

Distractedly, Munday said, 'Yes. We... we sent someone out to try and fetch help.'

'Your daughter,' O'Brien guessed.

Momentarily surprised that O'Brien should know such a fact, the horse trader nodded wretchedly. 'God knows if she got through. We can only pray.'

Eben cleared his throat to attract their attention. He was well advanced in years, short and skinny and bewhiskered, in a collarless white shirt and grey California pants held up by wide suspenders. 'That's how come you got through unchallenged, then, young feller. Haven's men were all likely chasing off after Laurel.'

He threw an uneasy glance up and over the surrounding hills, with their ragged ridges of brittle-looking timber. 'Maybe we'd ought to get you in off the street before someone up there spots you.'

Munday shook off his obvious filial concerns. 'Eben's right. And if I might be allowed a personal comment, the pair of you look as if you could do with some good strong coffee and a bait of home-cooked food.'

O'Brien nodded. 'Thanks.'

While Eben took care of their horses, Munday led them across the street towards the clustered townsfolk. A woman came down off the boardwalk to meet them halfway, tall, trim and handsome in a blue cotton dress and a lace-edged shawl.

154

She wore her brown hair centre-parted and pinned in a bun, and she, like all of them, showed strain around her blue eyes and firm mouth. Munday introduced her as his wife, Catherine. Then, as the rest of the citizenry split up into little groups and gradually drifted away, the Mundays led them down an alley towards the residential part of town, and into a neat frame cottage bordered by a low white picket fence.

'I can't offer you as much of a breakfast as I'd like,' Mrs Munday said apologetically. 'Shut away like this, we haven't been able to fetch in any supplies for a while, but I'll do my best.'

'We'd hate to rob you, ma'am,' said O'Brien.

'Don't you worry about that, Mr O'Brien. We'll find what we can. We're getting good at that around here.'

The Munday home was small and clean. The walls had been boarded over and papered, and the hallway, parlour and kitchen were filled with heavy pieces of furniture. Terry was yawning by the time they took chairs in the parlour and Mrs

Munday bustled off to the kitchen to see what she could rustle up. O'Brien wanted sleep as well, but that could wait.

They skirted around the main reason for O'Brien's visit for a while. Munday wanted to know how his brother was keeping, what had been going on in the outside world these past few months, and O'Brien answered him as best he could. Then Mrs Munday called them to the table and he and Terry wrapped themselves around a meal that was both appetising and, considering the circumstances, surprisingly substantial. As usual, Terry was there at O'Brien's side the minute he showed difficulty cutting into his bacon, and he coloured furiously as she mothered him, but he was grateful to her too, because her intentions were good, she only wanted to please and help him, to make him glad that he had bought her along after all.

Some time later, once they had finished, O'Brien pushed his plate away and said, 'All right, Mr Munday. What's this all about?'

Munday took a pipe from the mantel,

stuffed it with tobacco then fired it up. He looked at them through his troubled hazel eyes, wondering where to begin. At last he said, 'Do you feel up to a walk, Mr O'Brien?'

'Sure.'

Munday looked at Terry. She was stifling another yawn, practically out on her feet. 'Will you excuse us, Miss Olsen?'

Before Terry could respond, Mrs Munday linked arms with her. 'Of course you will, won't you, dear?'

O'Brien watched the girl. She wasn't used to being called "Miss", and she sure wasn't used to any great displays of affection. Though he was not usually given to sentiment, it nonetheless gave him a warm feeling inside to see how much it meant to her now. But she, like O'Brien, was curious.

'I'd like to come along with you, if you don't mind.'

'Of course.' Munday indicated that the two of them should precede him out of the house, and once they were back in the growing sunshine, they retraced their steps

157

to the street. This time, Rock View looked a little more alive. A few people were going about their business as best they could, and here and there a few had stopped to chat or eye the newcomers curiously when they thought they weren't looking. But there was still something wrong with the scene, something O'Brien could not immediately define, but which continued to nag at him as they walked on.

Munday led them down toward the end of the street, and from there up the gentle, brushy slope upon which the Rock View cemetery had been laid out. Finally, standing there with the town below them and a veritable forest of headstones pushing up out of the mounded earth all around, the horse trader said, 'To answer your question, Mr O'Brien—*this* is what it's all about.'

Terry frowned. 'A cemetery?'

'What lies below the cemetery. Below it, and inside this mountain.' Munday took his pipe from his mouth and released a cloud of smoke, which was swiftly shredded by the warm breeze.

O'Brien hazarded a guess. 'Silver?'

'Copper.'

'And Haven wants the copper?'

Munday nodded. 'Oh, Haven wants it, all right. That man has dedicated his entire life to the discovery and procurement of copper. His given name is Alex, but those who know him best call him by his nickname, "Red Metal". That's how closely the two are linked together.'

'Who is he, then, this Haven?' asked Terry.

'That's pretty much what I asked myself when he first arrived here five, six months ago, and started carrying out all those odd little geological tests of his. At first he tried to kid us on that he was some kind of an archaeologist. Oh, he didn't come right out and say so, not in so many words, but that's certainly the impression he gave. It was only when he finally started making noises about bringing prosperity to Rock View and promising us the moon if only we'd cooperate with him that I thought I'd better travel down to Mexican Hat and see what I could dig up on him.'

It was O'Brien's turn. 'And what did you find?'

'Firstly, that he was nothing whatever to do with archaeology, but a whole darn lot to do with mining. He's an engineer by trade. You know, he builds things. Evidently he drifted west after the war and ended up in Montana. That's where he first developed an interest in mining. About ten, eleven years ago, he raised enough money through some backers in England to stake a claim on a mountain just like this one, near Butte. He thought he was going to make his fortune in gold and silver back then, and he *did* get some silver out of that hill, but mostly what he got was copper, a lot of it—and at that time copper was one of the things this country was learning that it just couldn't do without. So he made a fortune—but not without cost.

'And that's the second thing I found out about him: that he's a hard man, in or out of business, and that he always plays to win. I don't know how many men he allowed to die down there in those stinking little tunnels of his back in Montana, but it was a whole lot, Mr O'Brien. Those that weren't drowned when the tunnels flooded were killed when they hit pockets of boiling water and scalding steam at the lower elevations. If they hadn't gone on strike when they did and refused to continue digging, Haven wouldn't have done a single thing to improve their safety down there. But they *did* strike, and so he designed and built an extra tunnel that not only drained all the others but also gave them additional ventilation as well.

'There's no two ways about it—it was a brilliant feat of engineering. But you see, here's my point. Haven would have happily let those men go on dying, so long as they got his precious "red metal" out of the ground for him. That's all that matters to him. It made him a rich man, and in turn he's become obsessed with it.'

'So what happened when he came to you?'

'He requested a meeting with the town council, which I duly arranged. I won't lie to you: he offered us very generous terms if we would allow him to tear up our cemetery, re-inter all the displaced coffins elsewhere, and open a shaft into the mountain from which he could commence a new mining operation. This, evidently, was the most practical spot for the purpose, since the rest of the mountain's base is comprised of solid rock.'

O'Brien nodded his understanding. 'And you said no?'

'That's right. He thought at first that we were trying to hold out for a better deal. Then he assumed that we just didn't want Rock View turned into a rough-and-ready mining camp. And he was certainly right about that. But not once did he give any consideration to the fact that we simply did not want our dead disturbed.'

He turned his back on the headstones and indicated the town. 'Do you see anything missing down there, Mr O'Brien?' he asked. 'Miss Olsen?'

O'Brien followed his gaze and, after a while, nodded. 'I don't see any school-house,' he noted cautiously. 'And I don't see any young folks. Meaning no offence, Mr Munday, but all I see are old-timers—some of them old before their time.'

Munday inclined his head. 'You don't miss much, then. But Rock View wasn't always like that. When we first came here, we had a dream, all of us. Nothing grand or ambitious, just a genuine desire to live a good, charitable life and raise our children according to God's Holy Word.

'But that was not to be, as we soon found out. We came here young and visionary, and in time we multiplied. Life was good to us. But then one day one of our children fell ill. Our doctor diagnosed a mild infection. But it spread through the young ones quickly and completely. Some of the adults contracted it as well, a couple died, though most survived it, with careful and constant nursing.

'Turned out it was diphtheria, a particularly baneful strain of it. The children... well, they never stood a chance. They just weren't strong enough to fight it. So they died. One by one...they died. My wife and I, we lost two boys. For many families, the loss was even greater than that. For some reason I have never been able to fathom, my daughter Laurel was spared. But she was the only one.

'So, the other children died and we buried them here. And in a way, we buried ourselves here, as well. A lot of folks left town, hoping to pick up their lives again elsewhere. But most of us stayed, just to be near...' He glanced around them. 'Just to be near this.'

'That's why we won't have Haven and his men digging this place up. Because we figure our children suffered enough in their young lives, without suffering the defilement of exhumation as well.'

Munday fell silent and O'Brien considered what he had said. He had never married and raised a family, so he could not fully imagine what it must be like to lose a child. But wasn't it morbid to spend a lifetime in mourning? Was it not an affront to the very God Munday professed to worship?

It wasn't for him to say, of course. He had not come here to pass judgement. But then, neither had he come expecting any of this.

'I take it you explained the...situation...to Haven?'

Munday turned to face them. 'Of course. But Haven isn't all that long on sentiment. He offered us a bigger financial settlement, and we said no. Then he showed his true colours, and told us we'd be sorry if we tried to block his plans.' Munday's lips twitched in a brief smile of recollection. 'That's when I told him to go to hell.

'But he's been wearing us down, O'Brien. Slowly, but surely. He dismantled the telegraph wires, effectively cutting us off from the rest of the territory. Then he brought in some roughnecks from Butte, and strung an invisible cord around us. Now, nothing—practically nothing—gets in or out of town. We're running low on supplies. Haven's twin gunmen, Ed and Gene Canfield, come in regularly to intimidate us. The pressure's mounting on the town council to give in to him. But you know as well as I do that the minute we sign whatever papers he's had drawn up to make his mining operation here all nice and legal, we lose everything. *Everything.'*

O'Brien nodded. Even if the people of Rock View gave Haven the permission he needed to start mining, they would still remain prisoners here, for Haven could never risk letting them stray far from town again, lest they attempt to expose his crooked, strong-arm tactics to the authorities in neighbouring Mexican Hat.

Continue to defy him or submit to his will—it was a simple enough choice. And yet these people could not win, no matter what they decided to do.

'All you can do, then,' Terry said at length, 'is hope your daughter can fetch help while your people have still got it in them to resist.'

Munday impatiently brushed his fringe back out of his eyes. 'Yes,' he agreed soberly. 'All we can do is hope. And pray.'

But even as he said it, someone in the street below came hustling towards them in a kind of shambling trot, waving his arms wildly to attract their attention, and as they turned to face the man and recognised him as old Eben, he yelled urgently up to them, *John! John! Riders comin' in!'*

SIX

They descended the gentle slope in a rush, Munday in the lead, O'Brien and Terry fetching up the rear. O'Brien sensed expectancy and fear riding the warm mid-morning breeze, and it did not surprise him, for in this land and at this time, the approaching riders could only signify trouble.

As the ground beneath them gave way to the hardpack of the street, the men and the girl saw the riders Eben had indicated coming in from the south and west, grouped together and still a considerable way out.

Townsfolk had started to gather in anxious little knots along the sidewalks.

Storekeepers came out into the street, hands raised to shield their eyes from the sun above as they squinted off into the distance. A few of them, spying Munday, headed for him on the double, no doubt seeking guidance and, perhaps, reassurance.

Munday turned to O'Brien and Terry, jamming his by-now cold pipe into a shirt pocket. His face had a tight, pinched look. His stable was right behind them, and he indicated it with a swift jab of the finger. 'Might be best if you two stay out of sight,' he said in a low voice.

O'Brien was inclined to agree. It would do no harm to keep their presence in town a secret, at least for the time being. In a situation as touchy as the one in which these people now found themselves, you had to take every advantage you could get. With a nod, he took Terry by the hand and headed for the stable. Behind them, the storekeepers descended upon Munday, voicing worried questions as they came.

The stable was filled with brown shadows, and like all such buildings, it smelled heavily of hay and horseflesh. Quickly, O'Brien scanned the place. A narrow board walkway led down between the double line of stalls to a corral out behind the place where horses, their own included, were milling contentedly. Their saddles and gear, he saw, had been stacked on a low pole just outside Munday's cluttered little office at the rear of the barn.

O'Brien and Terry took up a position just inside the big entranceway at the front of the building, so that they would be hidden from the newcomers, who had by this time entered Main and were eating up the ground at a steady, challenging walk.

Munday and the five townsmen who had come to join him were peering up the street, trying to identify them. After a moment, Munday made a kind of groaning noise, and a murmur rippled through his companions.

Alerted by this, O'Brien shifted a little sideways, so that he could view the street better through a gap between one weathered plank and the next.

He recognised the cowboy twin, Gene

Canfield, and two of the carbine-toting roughnecks who'd been with Haven the previous night. He identified them now from their build, the way they dressed, the bloodless, squinty look of them, as miners: men who had doubtless worked for Haven up in Butte, men who could use a pick-axe or a pick-handle with equal skill.

Then O'Brien caught his breath, for draped across Canfield's lap was a girl in a torn hickory shirt and blue pants. Her hands were tied behind her and her booted ankles were similarly bound with a length of waxed rope. He could not see her face, it was hidden beneath the hang of her thick, curly blonde hair, but he knew without a shadow of doubt that she was Laurel Munday.

Gene Canfield and the others came on at their unhurried walk. Gene was no longer wearing his canvas jacket. It was rolled and tied behind his cantle. O'Brien saw that he was surprisingly muscular, and a natural horseman. After another minute or so, he angled his mount towards the big barn and reined in before the assembled townsmen, the two men with him riding awkwardly to either side and a little to the rear.

A cold smile yanked Gene's washed-out, round face into an entirely new shape, and O'Brien saw an unpleasant glitter in his brown-but-very-nearly-black eyes as he surveyed them from beneath the shade of his tan J.B. 'Got a little package for you here, Munday,' he said. 'You know, you really shouldn't let anything wearing your brand stray so far off the home range.'

Munday's fists clenched and unclenched at his sides. His lips were working silently: he was mumbling his daughter's name.

Without ceremony, Gene grabbed a fistful of the girl's shirt and pulled her backwards, so that she spilled off the horse and landed awkwardly on her back with a little cry.

'Laurel!'

'Daddy...'

Now, as her flaxen hair tumbled back away from her face, it was revealed to O'Brien. He saw large, well-spaced hazel eyes, showing hurt now, a tilted nose, a strong, powerful mouth and a small but firm jaw. She was about Terry's age, twenty or so, but she looked much younger, possibly because of all the smudges and dried tear-tracks on her cheeks.

Munday said the girl's name again and went forward to sit her up and check her for injuries, but when he was near enough, Gene shook one foot free of the stirrup and struck out, booting him in the shoulder and shoving him backwards, away from her again.

Munday staggered and would have fallen if the men with him hadn't reached out to steady him. Even so, he very nearly went down.

'Daddy!'

Gene dismounted in one fluid motion and left his split reins trailing. On the surface he was all cowboy, that one, from his good, multi-purpose saddle to the warp of the long legs beneath his shotgun *chaparejos*. And yet O'Brien sensed that he was only playing at the part. There was no need for chaps in this country. His sidearm, a Remington Army .44, was a big, killing kind of gun, not the lighter, more practical, work-scarred weapon of a cow-puncher. And he wore it real low, the way a gunfighter would.

'That was a damned stupid thing you did, Munday,' Gene said with a disapproving shake of the head. 'Sending your little girl out to do your dirty work for you.' He tutted. 'She didn't get no further than a dozen miles before we picked her up. You're lucky she didn't get herself killed, way she was riding. And you're damned lucky indeed that Mr Haven decided to send her back in one piece.'

'*Damn you!*' Munday hissed. 'If you've harmed her in any way—'

Gene struck out again, fast as a snake, and hit him on the jaw. Munday's head jerked sideways and he sagged again, until the other men caught him.

In the barn, O'Brien's left hand clenched into a fist and his lips compressed. He had never stood by while another man, a man unable to defend himself, took lumps. But he was all too aware of his limitations now. The arm in the sling around his neck seemed to weigh a ton. It was useless to him.

Outside, Gene said, 'You been warned, Munday. And that goes for all of you. Go along with Mr Haven and you got no more worries. Go against him, go against any of us, and we'll crush you like ticks. Now, that's simple enough to understand, isn't it? But it seems like some people only ever learn by example. And you know what, Munday?' he asked. 'You've just been elected *today's* example.'

He came in again, grabbed the stable-owner by his shoulders, hauled him away from the rest of the men and hit him in the belly. Munday grunted and went up on the tips of his boots.

Eben cursed and took a step forward. 'Why, you mean-hearted—' But he froze when Gene's companions brought their saddleguns around on him.

The rest of the townsmen stood immobile, frozen by fear and a morbid fascination for the tableau being enacted before them. Only Laurel still tried to help, tried vainly to escape her bonds and struggle to her feet.

Gene let Munday fall to the dust, and when the stable-owner had collapsed at his feet, he kicked him in the stomach.

'Daddy!' Laurel's voice was filled with anguish, her throat tight as she fought to hold back fresh tears. 'Please...Canfield... You...you've made your point!'

Gene turned around and gave her a cool smile. 'You reckon?' He peered down at Munday, who was hunched up now, holding himself and wheezing softly behind clamped teeth. 'That right, Munday? You and your people gonna sign Mr Haven's papers now?'

Munday turned his head and glared up at the younger man. From the look of his expression, even Gene was surprised by the hard, flinty depth of hatred he saw in the stable-owner's eyes. Blood had spread across Munday's chin from a split in his lip. His fringe was stuck to his forehead in sweaty rats'-tails and he was breathing hard. Forcing himself up into a sitting position he pulled down a deep breath and husked, 'I'll...tell you what I...told your boss, Canfield. *Go to hell!'*

Gene shook his head in mock reproof. 'Now, that's not the answer I want to hear, Munday, and you know it.' His sigh was heavy and theatrical. 'Looks like I got to start all over again, don't it?'

And he kicked Munday in the stomach one more time.

Back in the shadows, O'Brien had seen enough. On impulse he headed for the door. Taken by surprise, Terry whispered his name, but he paid her no heed. He pushed out into the sunshine and on through the line of townsmen, not sure what he was going to do, not sure exactly what he *could* do, knowing only that these people could expect no help from Mexican Hat now, that unless they were taught to resist and resist with force and in no uncertain terms, this siege would go on and on and in the end they would spend whatever remained of their lives firmly under Haven's control.

Gene was just about to draw his foot back for another kick when he caught a movement from the edge of his vision and looked up. Surprise registered on his face for a second, if that, and then he seemed to forget all about Munday and grinned. 'Well, well,' he said. 'If it isn't my friend with the busted arm. You're a little off-course, aren't you? I thought you said you was headed for Mexican Hat?'

O'Brien said, 'And I thought your boss said there was no such town as Rock View.'

Gene shrugged. 'Well, before you get any fancy notions, mister, I'll say it plain. Stay out of this. It's none of your concern.'

O'Brien looked at him, into his eyes. Up close, Gene's skin had the look of unbaked dough, and was mottled with very pale freckles. Very quietly he said, 'I'm *making* it my concern, cowboy.'

He knew it was a stupid thing to do. He knew that the whole thing might blow up in his face and that it might end up causing more trouble than it would solve. But it didn't appear that there was anyone else around here with guts enough to stand up to these bully-boys. So...

He smashed Gene right in the face with

his bunched left fist and Gene made a kind of smacking sound with his lips and lurched backwards, reaching for his bloodied nose.

As one, the assembled townsmen gasped. Up on their horses, the two men who had accompanied Gene into town made to bring their carbines around on him. O'Brien had expected that, of course, and was just about to reach into his sling for his Colt when suddenly Terry snapped, 'Throw down them rifles if you want to stay alive!' and O'Brien, not daring to look behind him at her, heard her jack a shell into his Winchester, and knew that she had gone and fetched it from his gear with the express intention of backing whatever play he made.

He glanced from one of the miners to the other. They were scowling at the girl, trying to decide whether or not she meant what she said, figuring that she probably did, and after a moment one of them swore as only a miner could, then threw his weapon off to the side, and almost immediately his companion did likewise.

That was all O'Brien had been waiting for.

He stepped over Munday and closed the gap towards Gene quickly, because Gene had recovered a bit by now and, ignoring his streaming nose, was reaching for his gun. Just as the gun cleared leather, O'Brien crowded him in and swatted it aside, and it spun through the air a couple of times, then hit the ground with a dull thud.

Gene looked into O'Brien's face then, right into his eyes. Whatever he saw there did not alarm him, it scared the pants off him. He opened his mouth to speak but before he could say anything, O'Brien hit him again.

The punch snapped Gene's head back. He toppled to one side and O'Brien went right after him, knowing he'd be fine as long as Gene wasn't able to get in any licks of his own, or go for his one liability, the busted arm.

Confused and disoriented, Gene was back-pedalling to put distance between himself and O'Brien and give himself a chance to recover. O'Brien saw desperation in every jerky move that he made.

Gene was swearing and trying to sleeve the blood from his face all in one. O'Brien came in again and hit him a third time, taking advantage of his mental and physical imbalance, not liking it but knowing it had to be done, and his fist made a wet, pulpy sound when it connected with Gene's jaw.

Gene swore again and bent double. He made a choking sound and when he opened his mouth a stringy length of blood and saliva stretched from his lips to the ground.

There was still some fight left in him, though. With a yell he swung a left hook. O'Brien leaned back, away from it, and it caught only the muggy afternoon air. Gene bawled, *'You bastard!'* and followed it up with a right. O'Brien dodged that too, brought his left knee up and caught the twin hard in the belly.

Gene went, 'Ahhh...' as the air went out of him. He wobbled a bit, his arms and legs hanging loose, and O'Brien hit him again, once more, again for good measure.

Gene was weaving and stumbling on legs like jelly. He was putty in O'Brien's hands —or, to be more accurate, in O'Brien's hand. His eyes were glazing fast and his lips were starting to swell. At last he collapsed to his knees, and because he wanted these men to learn their lesson well, O'Brien finished him off with a kick in the belly.

Gene flipped over backwards and sprawled on the ground, breathing hard and whining.

Breathing hard himself, O'Brien turned to face the miners. They were sitting their fidgety horses in grim silence, their bearded, brawl-scarred faces impassive. He looked into their eyes, knowing that he would find the true nature of their shielded emotions there, and sure enough, he saw uncertainty, anger and frustration.

'Right,' he said quietly.

One of the men said, 'If it's another fight you want, you've come to the right man here, bucko. Don't make no never-mind to me that you only got the use o' one arm.'

A tic of a smile skimmed across O'Brien's mouth. His only intention had been to tell these two to put Gene back on his horse and get the hell out of town. But if they still wanted to fight, he'd better oblige them or back down, and he could hardly back down now, otherwise this entire exhibition would have been for nothing.

'All right,' he said. 'Come ahead if you've a mind to.'

The man threw a cautious glance at Terry, then swung down. He was big and muscular, six feet even and as wide as a door, with a nose that had gone walkabout on his face, a couple of chipped teeth and the puffy eyes of a pug. He came at O'Brien like he could hardly wait to get started, pushing up the sleeves of his old brown jacket as he did so.

O'Brien stood in the centre of the street, waiting for him to come. He could feel the eyes of every man and woman there upon him. They were wondering how he was going to hold his own against this heavier man, laid up as he was. And, he had to admit, he was kind of wondering about that himself.

He waited for the miner to come a little nearer, and when he judged that the man was close enough, he pulled the Colt from his sling and brought it up and around in a vicious arc.

The barrel caught the oncoming man on the side of the face and the sight opened up a gash on his whiskery cheek and knocked loose another couple of his teeth. The miner, taken completely by surprise, gave a howl, but O'Brien showed him no mercy. This was not the time for mercy. Like it or not, he had to fight as mean and dirty as these sons if he was to make any kind of a point at all.

He struck the miner across the face again, and when the man reached up to hold his ruined mouth together, he kicked him right in the happy-sacks and the miner went up, then down, and rolled around on the ground, clutching his groin.

O'Brien stood back then, and glanced from the miner to Gene.

Even if he said so himself, it wasn't

a bad performance for a man with a broken arm.

He fixed the third man with a hard look. The man, thinking that O'Brien was going to administer some of the same treatment to him, began to shake his head. But O'Brien had had his fill of violence. He was a professional fighting man. That was how he made his way in the world. But it was a job. And you only worked at your job as long as you had to.

'Get your buddies on their horses and then get them out of town,' he said. 'And when you get back to camp, tell Haven he's pushed these people far enough, and that he'd better not try to push them any further if he knows what's good for him.'

Regaining some of his mettle now that he knew the fighting was over, the miner said, 'That's real fine talk, mister. But you're a fool if you think you'll get away with this.'

'Well then, maybe I ought to put it another way,' O'Brien said mildly. 'The next time you or your bully-boy friends come into town figuring to ride roughshod over these people, you'd better come expecting trouble, cause sure enough that's what you're going to get.'

'What's that supposed to mean?'

O'Brien smiled coolly. 'Try it and find out,' he invited.

He backed off a few paces and all of them watched as the miner dismounted and set about trying to get his companions back onto their feet and across to their horses. Neither Gene nor the man O'Brien had pistol-whipped were in any condition to cause further trouble, at least for the time being, so some of the tension electrifying the air began to evaporate.

'How...how about givin' me a hand, here?' the miner called over one shoulder as he struggled to hoist Gene across his hull.

O'Brien glanced along the line of townsmen. It appalled him that only one of them had tried to go to Munday's aid. He singled out a fat storekeeper in an apron and green sleeve-protectors and said, 'Give him a hand, mister.'

The man looked at him bug-eyed. 'M-me?'

Munday regained his feet and took out a kerchief with which to staunch the flow of blood at his lip. 'Yes, Frank, *you,*' he said a trifle testily. 'The sooner they get mounted, the sooner we get them out of our town.'

Eben paused in the act of collecting up the discarded carbines, and not for the first time, O'Brien felt that he'd found an ally in the thin, white-whiskered old-timer. 'Hell, I'm all for that,' he said, propping the saddlebags up against the stable wall and spitting into the palms of his hands. 'Come on, Frank, I'll give you a hand.'

As the three Haven men rode slowly out of town, Munday's wife came hurrying across the street towards them, no doubt having been alerted to the trouble by a neighbour. For a long time she and her husband fussed tearfully around their daughter. O'Brien watched as they untied her, listened to their anxious questions and her steady replies as she sought to convince them that she was all right.

He felt the eyes of the other townsmen on him, and returned their appraisal. He hadn't done what he had in order to ingratiate himself with them, or show what a swell fellow he was. He didn't especially want their gratitude or adoration. He'd wanted only to save John Munday from taking some undeserved punishment.

So he was a bit surprised by the open animosity he saw them directing his way now.

Wryly he told himself, *If looks could kill...* But this was no joke. *He* wasn't the enemy here. He had tried only to help. And yet, as he looked at them now, and they hurriedly turned away from him rather than meet his gaze, there was no mistaking their resentment.

He put his .38 back into his sling, feeling short on patience. It made him feel uncomfortable to think that maybe he *had* over-stepped the mark, taken too much upon himself. After all, who did he think he was? What gave him the right to speak for the entire town?

Terry came over, his Winchester cradled in her arms. She looked pale beneath her tan, and shaken up by the recent confrontation. He offered her a crooked smile as, around them, the storekeepers and townsfolk began to drift away, some of them still casting murderous glances his way.

'Thanks, girl,' he said, indicating the long gun. 'That's another one I owe you.'

To his surprise, she only tossed her head in a gesture of dismissal. 'You think I like seein' you risk your life like that?' she asked angrily. 'Is that it?'

Without waiting for a reply, she turned on her heel and disappeared back into the stable, and he followed her with his eyes, feeling vaguely bewildered. Somehow, all of this was getting away from him. He couldn't do right for doing wrong. Again he felt the enormous, dead weight of his gun-arm. He felt impotent without the use of it, unable to truly gain control of the situation.

The Mundays led their daughter across

the street, towards home. With a lop-sided shrug, he told himself that there would be time enough for a more formal introduction later. Right now, he figured he might as well book him and Terry into the hotel, and went to fetch the redhead from the rear of the building.

She was standing with her back to him, watching the horses roll and nudge each other in the corral. He could tell she'd been crying. Something had upset her, something more than just their confrontation with Haven's men. He thought about asking her what it was, then decided to say nothing. She would tell him soon enough, if she was of a mind to.

Apart from a couple of permanent boarders, theirs became the only names in the hotel register. The woman who owned and ran the place, a matronly though still quite glamorous lady in her late fifties, gave them adjoining rooms on the first floor. The rooms were clean enough, but had an air of long disuse. Still, they did at least offer a good view of the street below, and that, O'Brien decided, might have its uses.

He watched Terry go wordlessly to her room. He could not understand what had gotten into her, and frankly was too tired and edgy to give it much immediate thought. She was of a fickle and unfathomable sex, he thought. And, because of the times in which he lived, he was content to put whatever the true nature of her problems might be down to the pure and simple fact that she was, above all else, a woman.

The first thing he did when he closed his room door behind him was bathe the knuckles of his left hand in the bowl of cold water that was sitting on the washstand. In a fight you normally shared the blows out between both fists, but O'Brien had had to restrict all his punches to his left hand alone, and now it throbbed like a bitch.

He looked out into the distance, across the shallow, scrubby basin and up across the slopes to the dried-out trees rising just back from the craggy rims. The morning was waning, the climbing sun a bloated orange ball hanging high in the cerulean sky.

When he was through tending to his hand, he took off his hat and boots, removed his .38 and put it on the dresser, then stretched out on the bed. It renewed him just to close his eyes and relax his muscles.

In a peace broken only occasionally by one innocent town-sound or another, he thought about what Munday had told him up at the cemetery. Again it troubled him that these people had given their whole lives over to mourning the dead, that instead of making something positive out of the here and now, they had chosen to remain lodged stubbornly in the past. Yet he reminded himself that whatever they chose to do, that was up to them. It was none of his affair.

That made him consider his own next move. He had come here to find out why Doc Munday's brother had suddenly stopped writing to him. Well, he'd done that, all right. But what should he do next?

Just what *could* a man incapacitated as he was *do?*

He flexed the fingers of his right hand, just to keep them working, and thought about spending another five weeks with his gun-arm in a sling. The prospect galled him. At last he drifted off to sleep and the day matured around him until morning finally gave way to late afternoon.

When he woke up again it was five o'clock and he had a headache, for the room had grown hot and stuffy during the course of the day, but he felt refreshed as well. He sat up, hauled his boots back on with some difficulty, tucked his gun back into his sling, then left the room and went next door to find Terry.

When she answered his knock, he saw that she too had rested well. She had fixed her hair and changed her clothes, and the heat of the day had put a rose in each of her cheeks, making her look good. But when he suggested they go get something to eat, her subdued response told him that her sudden bleak mood was still upon her.

They went down to the restaurant three doors along and were served up some stringy chicken and watery mashed potato. Right the way through the meal, Terry was uncharacteristically close-mouthed. No matter how many times he tried to draw her out, she remained quiet.

Outside the street darkened, and amber lights began to glow behind thick lace curtains. Rock View held itself hushed and expectant beneath star and moon. O'Brien paid the tab, and then they walked back to the hotel. There, O'Brien saw Terry to her shadowed room, and while he searched around for matches with which to get her lamp working, she suddenly said, 'You know you could have got yourself killed this afternoon.'

Slowly he turned to face her, temporarily abandoning his hunt for a match, sensing that she was finally going to get whatever it was out of her system, and that it might be easier for her if she was given the darkness behind which to hide at least some of her feelings.

'Is that what's troubling you?' he asked

193

gently. 'What's *really* troubling you, I mean?'

Defensively she snapped, 'You think that's not enough, watchin' someone you care about tryin' his damndest to get himself killed? Or were you just showin' off?'

'Showing off?'

'For *her* benefit. Laurel.'

He put a note of warning in his voice. 'Hey, now...'

He reached for her but she shrugged out of his grip, then changed her mind. 'Aw, I didn't mean that. It's just...I don't know...'

O'Brien said, 'You missing the old life?'

She hunched up her shoulder. 'No. Yes. Aw, I...' He watched as she wrung her moon-silvered hands. 'I miss *part* of it. You know. The lights, the laughter, the occasional drink. Bein' wanted. But nothin' else. You know. Not the men. It's just...you get used to it. You know. Feelin' wanted. Loved. Even though you know it's not real love, that it don't last no longer'n takes a man to...well, you know. At least you feel wanted.'

194

'Do you want to go back to it?' he asked carefully.

Her response was adamant. 'Heck, no. Never. I finished with all that. And I ain't never been treated so well anywhere else in my life. That Catherine, she's real nice. I like her a lot. It just...takes a little gettin' used to. The quiet. 'Specially after what I been used to.'

He nodded. 'Get an early night,' he suggested. 'Tomorrow's another day.'

He got as far as the door and then she said his name, softly, tentatively, with a little, desperate catch in her throat, and she made it sound like an invitation.

He turned back to her. Around them, the hotel was very quiet. In the faint light filtering in through the window, he saw her reach up and begin to unbutton her shirt. He had known for a long time that she wanted him. He was surprised to find that he wanted her. She finished unbuttoning the shirt and pulled the tails out from her waistband.

She was wearing nothing underneath.

O'Brien swallowed, his throat tight,

paradoxically wondering how in hell he was going to manage this, his right arm being bandaged up and all. He went over to her and put his left palm on her shoulder and squeezed, and he lowered his head and was just about to kiss her when he heard a floorboard creak in the hallway outside, and someone knocked at the door.

O'Brien felt Terry deflate a little beneath his hand. Then she turned away from him and began to rebutton her shirt, and he knew that the moment had well and truly been broken. Whoever was out there knocked again, and O'Brien went over to the door and opened it, just a little.

He was surprised to find Laurel Munday awaiting him. The girl looked up at him through very serious hazel eyes and said, 'Mr O'Brien? I'm sorry, I hope I'm not interrupting...anything. It's just that I heard voices and...'

She trailed off, suspecting what she had disturbed and not really knowing what else to say, and to fill the silence he said,

'Forget it. We haven't been introduced yet, but—'

'My father's told me all about you,' she said, extending her hand. 'He...that is, the town council, would like to see you. They're down at our house right now.'

He didn't know what to read into that, but if the looks he'd received earlier were any indication, he was sure it could mean nothing good. 'I'll be there in about ten minutes,' he told her.

She was trying to peer over his shoulder and see into the darkened room. She looked a whole deal better than she had the last time he'd seen her. Her blonde hair was combed back off her clean-lined face and gathered into a pony-tail that reached to the small of her back. She stood five feet seven, with a figure that was all curves and swells beneath a check blouse and split brown riding skirt that ended just past her knees.

'I'll, ah...wait for you downstairs, then,' she said. 'We might as well walk back together.'

'Sure.'

A few minutes later, O'Brien and Terry came downstairs and O'Brien made the introductions. At first Terry was a bit guarded. She was afraid that Catherine or her daughter might have suspected something of her past and intended to condemn her for it, but Laurel put her at ease right away with complete and unquestioning acceptance, and O'Brien half-suspected that she was just glad to have some company of her own age after spending all these years surrounded by elders.

As they headed back to the Munday house, O'Brien said, 'You're probably sick and tired of people asking, Laurel, but...how are you feeling now?'

She gave a strained little smile. 'Haven didn't treat me too badly, if that's what you mean.'

'It didn't look that way earlier on.'

'Oh, I'm not going to say that Haven's men were angels. That Gene Canfield...' and here a shudder ran through her. 'That man's got some strange ideas about women. But Haven kept him in line, thank God. He kept all of them in line.'

'Who *are* the Canfields?' asked Terry. 'Do you know?'

'Daddy says they're hired guns from New Mexico. Haven used them once before, to help him break a miners' strike in Montana, and he drafted them in again a couple of months ago to help him intimidate *us*. It's the same with the rest of his hired thugs. They're strike-breakers. Bullies. Killers, too, I think.'

O'Brien indicated the way ahead. 'Do you know what they've been discussing tonight, the town council?'

She nodded. 'Yes. And for what it's worth, I think it's a rotten trick.'

'What is?'

They came in sight of the Munday house then, and Laurel, realising that she'd been thinking aloud, said, 'Maybe I'd better let them explain it. But take my word for it, Mr O'Brien. It's a rotten trick they've got planned for you. The rottenest.'

SEVEN

They went into the house and found a group of five elderly men sitting in the parlour, awaiting their arrival. As they entered the lamplit room, O'Brien recognised the men who had been with Munday that morning, when Gene Canfield had come to call. This, then, he thought, was the town council.

Munday himself was standing beside the mantel. As Laurel showed O'Brien and Terry into the room and gestured to a couple of vacant chairs which they declined, Munday nodded a greeting and O'Brien, indicating the man's scabbed and swollen lip, said, 'How does it feel?'

Munday said, 'Fine.' But he didn't look all that fine. In fact, he looked mad enough to spit.

For a time, the councillors regarded O'Brien and the redhead in stony silence.

Munday's wife came in with a fresh pot of coffee and cups for the newcomers. While she poured, Laurel crossed the room and stood beside her father. Over in the far corner, Eben stopped nibbling on a soda cracker and nodded a greeting. O'Brien gave him an answering wink.

At last Munday cleared his throat and spoke again. 'The town council thought we'd better have a word,' he said. 'About what happened this morning.'

O'Brien had expected that. 'Go on,' he said guardedly.

'Well, first of all, I want you to know that I appreciate what you did for me today,' Munday said uncomfortably. Clearly he was struggling with something inside of him. 'But, well, the town council has come to the conclusion that, in the long run, you didn't do us any favours by...taking a hand.'

'Oh?'

'No,' said the fat storekeeper Munday had referred to earlier as Frank. 'And if you can't understand why, I'll tell you. It's because you as good as declared war

201

out there this morning!'

'That's a bare-faced lie!' said Terry, outraged by the accusation.

'Easy, girl,' O'Brien said gently.

'Well, what was it, then, if it wasn't an out-and-out challenge for Haven to do his worst?' asked Frank.

O'Brien looked at him. He was a big-bellied man with a bald head surrounded by a fringe of white-grey hair. When he spoke, a cigar twitched up and down at the corner of his mouth. O'Brien looked at all the men of the town council, one at a time. Only in Munday, Munday's wife, his daughter and old Eben did he find any glimmer of support.

At last he put his gaze back on Frank and said, 'Can I ask you something?'

Momentarily surprised, Frank said, 'I guess.'

'Did any of you men put up any kind of resistance when Haven first came in here with his plan to take over your town? Any kind of resistance at all?'

No-one spoke. A couple of the men shuffled their feet uncomfortably.

'Well,' O'Brien said with a shake of the head, 'maybe if you had, you wouldn't be in this fix now.'

'Now see here,' began a tall, angular man with a liver-spotted forehead. 'Maybe you'd better take a closer look at us before you go passing judgement, O'Brien. You think we'd be much good in a fight? At our time of life?'

O'Brien said, 'All I'm saying is this—that Haven's not just going to give up and go away if he can't get what he wants, not if there's as much copper in that mountain of yours as he thinks there is. And he's not going to play this waiting game forever. Sooner or later you're going to have to fight him, to keep what's yours.

'Do you understand me? You can forget all about getting help from Mexican Hat. You're on your own in this, and the sooner you realise it, the better. And I'll tell you something else, as well. If Haven's men are as ruthless as Laurel here seems to think they are, you're going to have to fight like you've never fought before.'

'We've had our fill of death in this town,

Mr O'Brien,' said a fiftyish man in a grey suit and flat, townsman's shoes. 'We don't want any more.'

'I appreciate that. But sometimes you have to take a stand whether you want to or not.'

'Aw, what do you know about it?' Frank asked stubbornly.

'I know this much, mister,' O'Brien replied. 'Out here, life's all about one thing—getting up one more time than you're knocked down.'

He released his breath through his nose. It made a snake's hiss in the silence. Again he looked at the men facing him. Not one man there could meet his gaze. But he saw enough fear and genuine, gut-sick worry on their haggard faces to convince him that no amount of argument would bring them over to his way of thinking.

He put his cup of coffee down on the table, untouched, feeling a mixture of emotions. These people had been lucky to have gone as long as they had without having to fight to hold what was theirs. But now that luck had run out. The only language men like Haven understood was strength and determination. But so far, these isolated, insulated men and women of Rock View had shown him neither.

'All right,' he said at last, frustration making him sound tired. 'It's none of my affair. You people do whatever you think you ought to do.'

'And what about Haven?' demanded Frank. 'What's *he* going to do, after what you did today?'

O'Brien squinted at him, sensing that they were finally leading up to the rotten trick Laurel had warned him about. 'You got something to say,' he said quietly, 'say it.'

Frank glanced to left and right to make sure the others were still with him on this. Suddenly he was sweating. He said, 'We want you to ride out to Haven's camp at first light tomorrow and...and tell him you didn't mean what you said.'

O'Brien watched him with a poker face, and Frank squirmed under his steady stare.

'We...we want you to tell him that

whatever you did or said to antagonise his men this morning was done in the heat of the moment,' he went on. 'And...and that you weren't in any way acting on our behalf when you did it.'

O'Brien didn't speak at once, but he heard Terry whisper, *'What?'* Then, finding her voice, she said, 'You're not serious! You'd ask O'Brien to go out there an' eat crow after what he did to try an' *help* you?'

'Leave it, Terry,' O'Brien cautioned.

'Leave it, hell!' she said angrily. 'Sendin' you out there's as good as throwin' you to a pack of wolves, an' they know it!'

'You've got to understand the position here, lady,' said Frank. 'You come down to my store, take a look around. All you'll see are shelves that're darn-near empty, and my wife doing her best to make a little food go a long, long way. Hell, we didn't have much of a trade *before* Haven came to town, but now we've got nothing at all!'

'Is that all you're worried about?' Terry asked disdainfully. 'Your lousy turnover?'

'It's not just that,' said a man in a black suit, pausing to consult a heavy gold watch which he then tucked back into a vest pocket. 'You wouldn't know my situation. But to put it briefly, my wife...she's dying. And try as he might, Doc Harper here can't do anything to make her passing any easier, he just hasn't got enough supplies in his medicine chest.'

'That's right,' said the man in the grey suit, now identified as the town medico. 'We're hurting, all of us. Physically. Mentally. Financially. And it's getting worse with every passing day. We just can't afford to make the situation any worse. We've *got* to make amends with Haven.'

But Terry wasn't having any of that. 'You know your trouble, you people?' she asked. 'You make your reasons to fight sound more like excuses *not* to.'

'I think you've said enough, little missy!' snapped Frank.

She shook her head. 'I don't think I've said *half* enough, yet!' she countered. 'Mr Munday here, he told us all about how you lost your children, an' it was real sad, 'course it was. But once they was dead an' buried, you people just threw in the towel, 'stead of gettin' on with your lives. And you been throwin' in the towel ever since.'

Doc Harper went bright red. 'That's a *hell* of a thing to say!'

'It's true, though, isn't it?' Terry replied. 'You folks...maybe it's about time you remembered what it's like to stand up and fight—not just for your cemetery an' what it means to you, but to protect your wives an' your businesses...an' your town itself.'

Silence pressed in on the small office. A couple of the men squirmed uncomfortably, shamed by the truth of her words. But then the portly storekeeper said doggedly, 'When we need a doxy to tell us our business—'

O'Brien felt Terry stiffen and suck in a low, hurt breath beside him, and he said with quiet menace, 'Just keep using that mouth of yours, mister, that's all.'

Munday reached up to brush his fringe back off his forehead. 'All right, all right, let's just simmer down, now. This kind of bickering's not going to get us anywhere.'

For a moment O'Brien continued to hold Frank's eye with his own, while Munday waited impatiently for their tempers to cool. When he was sure that some kind of order had returned to the meeting, he sighed and said, 'That's better. Now... For what it's worth, Mr O'Brien, I'm with you on this. Trying to play Haven at this waiting game, forever turning the other cheek...it's got us nowhere, and it's not going to solve anything. I'm not a violent man, but I appreciate that, as you say, there are times when a man has to make a stand, no matter how offensive he might find it. And I've already made it plain to Frank and the others that I don't believe for one moment that you were so much declaring war on Haven today as trying to bring this entire affair to a head—which would be no bad thing.

'But I'm only one voice here. I can't say I approve of what Frank has asked you to do, but I have to bow to the wishes of the majority.'

O'Brien nodded. 'All right,' he said. 'I'll go see Haven first thing in the morning.'

Terry's eyes burned into him. 'O'Brien!'

'I guess I owe you people that much,' he went on. 'But if the ladies will pardon my language, I'm damned if I'll go with my tail between my legs, the way you want me to. You're right, Munday—it wasn't my intention to declare war. But with men like Canfield and those other rowdies, you talk straight and you talk tough, and if it comes to it, you back it up all the way, because if you don't, if you show them any sign of weakness at all, they'll come ahead and stamp right over you. You folks'll learn that in time, if you haven't already. And you'll learn it the hardest way there is.'

'Don't think we're proud of what we're asking you to do,' said Doc Harper, relenting a little.

'But standing up to me is easier than standing up to Haven, is that it?' O'Brien asked, lifting one eyebrow.

He touched his fingers to the brim of his hat and said, 'If that's all...' Then he turned around and strode out of there with Terry at his heels, thinking that Laurel hadn't been kidding when she'd said they were planning something rotten for him, knowing that they were as good as asking him to commit suicide on the morrow—and knowing that, dammit, that's just what he was going to do, too.

When they got back to the hotel, O'Brien saw Terry to her door and then made to turn away and head on towards his own room. The girl hadn't said a word on the short walk back from Munday's house, but now she reached up and put a hand on his arm and whispered, 'O'Brien. Tell me you're not really going through with it. What Munday and the others asked you to do.'

His answer was simplicity itself. 'I *said* I would, didn't—'

'But you can't!'

'Why not?'

'Haven won't let you get away with what you did to his men. He'll make an example out of you, he's bound to.

And if he doesn't, Canfield's sure to try and kill you himself!'

'We'll see.'

Desperation entered her voice. 'Listen, let's just leave here now, tonight. We could ride out under cover of darkness—'

'—and run smack into one of Haven's sentries?' he asked. 'That'd get us killed for sure.'

He felt her fingers knead the heavy muscles in his left arm and saw tears glistening wetly in her eyes. 'I don't want to lose you, O'Brien,' she whispered through twitching lips.

He looked down at her. Again she made him feel uneasy. He wanted to tell her that she shouldn't say a thing like that, because he wasn't really hers *to* lose. But he was taking her too seriously. She was probably just confusing gratitude with love and allowing her emotions to run away with her.

'Terry...'

'Shhh.'

She felt behind her with her free hand and opened the door to her room, then backed slowly into the darkness, the fingers of her other hand twisting into the material of his shirtsleeve and tugging him along after her. Slowly the darkness reached out and consumed them both, and a moment later O'Brien heeled the door shut behind him.

That night, Terry had all the love and attention she had ever wanted. But when she woke up next morning, O'Brien was gone.

He slipped out of bed shortly before dawn, while she was still asleep, and dressed as quickly and quietly as he could, so's not to wake her. As he buttoned his shirt one-handed, he looked down at her. In sleep she appeared tranquil and childlike, with her lustrous red head fanned out across the pillow beneath her. He looked down at her, remembering the night before. It had been good. Damned good. But was it love?

He felt old and tired and confused. It came to him without warning that he was nearly twice the age of the girl in the bed, and that made him feel older still. Maybe Munday's brother had been right when he'd said that O'Brien was getting too long in the tooth for the kind of life he led.

Then his mouth trimmed down and something altogether harder and more dangerous entered his eyes as he thought about what still lay ahead. He scooped the .38 up off the bedside cabinet, checked it and then stuffed it inside his sling.

It was time to be moving.

He left the room and closed the door with a soft click behind him. Around him, the hotel was enveloped in a web of silence and shadow. Only the occasional creak of a settling beam broke the pre-dawn solitude of the place.

He stepped out onto the street. Beneath a watery, charcoal-smudged sky, Rock View was a ghost town again. With a shiver, for the night cold still lingered, he set off up the street, headed for Munday's stable and his horse.

He let himself into the building, found a closed lantern hanging on a nail inside the doorway and lit it. Then he led the mustang out of his stall and set about trying to saddle up.

'Here,' said a voice behind him. 'I'll do that.'

He turned just as Eben came shuffling towards him from out of the darkened office at the rear of the barn. The old-timer was hatless, and his wispy hair, mussed from a night's restless sleep, was standing up around his ears. The tails of his collarless old shirt were hanging out of his grey pants, and his suspenders were twisted up around his shoulders. His walk was steady enough, but when he came close, O'Brien smelled home-brewed whiskey on his breath.

He nodded a greeting. 'Eben.'

Eben took the blanket from him, draped it across the horse's back and smoothed it out. Then he brushed past O'Brien and went to fetch his saddle from the pole outside the office. He had a frail look to him, as if he might blow away in a strong wind, but when he hefted the saddle and slung it up across the blanket, he made the thing seem hollow. With practised movements, he set about shouldering the air out of the animal so that he could tighten the twin girths.

'You work for Munday?' O'Brien asked.

Eben made a gesture. 'He lets me bunk in here. I do a few odd chores to pay my way.'

O'Brien flexed the fingers of his right hand some more, regretting the fact that he had never tried to teach himself to use his left with equal dexterity.

'So,' Eben said after a moment. 'You're goin' out there, like they ast.'

'Uh-huh.'

'Well, you got guts, I'll say that for you.' He glanced over his shoulder and O'Brien saw a wicked gleam in his rheumy eyes. ''Fact,' he said, 'I suspicion we'll be seein' 'em before the day's out.'

O'Brien took the rest of his tack down off a hook and passed it over. 'I hope *not.*'

'Uh, listen...' Eben said, suddenly awkward. 'What your woman said las' night, 'bout us folks throwin' in the towel when our young 'uns died.'

'What about it?'

'She was right. That's 'xactly what we did.' He fixed O'Brien with a sharp, questioning look. 'You understan' what I'm sayin', young feller?'

'Not really.'

Eben glanced beyond O'Brien to the open stable door, to make sure they wouldn't be overheard. 'I'm sayin' we ain't worth the sacrifice they're expectin' you to make, that's what I'm sayin'. I'm tellin' you to forget all about ridin' out to see Haven. Make a break for it. Try an' get away from here, an' take your woman with you.'

'She's not my woman.'

'No? Well, I seen the way she looked at you las' night, O'Brien. Maybe it's about time you *made* her your woman.'

O'Brien said nothing, just watched the old-timer finish saddling up for him. But Eben saw the smile playing in his eyes and said, 'I know, I know. Crazy old Eben. Don't pay him no mind. He's harmless enough, just a mite touched in the head.

But maybe old Eben's not as crazy as ever'one thinks. Maybe he knows more'n he lets on, eh?'

'Maybe he does at that,' O'Brien allowed.

The old man straightened up with a wince. 'There. All done.' He pulled at the big, rubbery lobe of his right ear, studying O'Brien all the while. At length he said, 'I got a couple ounces of mama's ruin left in my hip flask, if you'd care to partake.'

'No thanks.'

'Don't tell me you're temperance.'

'I'm sure not that. But I'd better keep a clear head.'

Eben nodded. 'Ay, maybe you'd better, at that.'

Suddenly something occurred to O'Brien and he said, 'You got a handgun I could borrow, Eben?'

Eben squinted at him. 'I got them carbines Haven's men left behind 'em yest'day.'

'No, I need a handgun.'

'I got that Canfield feller's .44.'

'That'll do fine.'

'I'll go fetch it. Picked it up after you sent them fellers away with a flea in their ears. Knew it'd come in handy.'

He fetched it and watched as O'Brien took out his Colt and stuffed it into the waistband of his cords, out of sight against the small of his back, then slipped the .44 into his sling, beside his bandaged arm.

He pulled at his ear some more, then, once O'Brien was finished, he said, 'Well...be honoured if you'd let me shake you by the hand, young feller.'

O'Brien said, 'Sure.' He extended his left hand and Eben ran his palm down his pants'-leg before reaching out to take it.

'If we had a few more like you around here,' the old man opined, 'We'd've whupped Haven a long time back.'

'You might just whup him yet,' O'Brien replied, not really believing it.

He toed in and mounted up. Out beyond the doors, light from the rising sun was slowly starting to accumulate.

'So long,' he said.

Eben said, 'Good luck.'

He rode out.

He left Rock View behind him and just kept going, not headed in any particular direction but knowing that sooner or later one of Haven's men would be bound to spot him and stop him and take him exactly where he wanted to go. And, sure enough, as he sent the mustang up the slope toward the timbered rims that hemmed the town in fifteen minutes later, a rider came out of the trees and onto the trail ahead to intercept him, holding a saddlegun across his lap.

O'Brien shortened his rein and slowed the horse, assessing the man ahead through cautious eyes. He was about thirty or so, squat and stubby, with wide sloping shoulders and a torso that strained the material of his grey workshirt. He had a flat, scarred face and stubble as thick and black as soot around his mouth and along his jaw. A green wool cap was pulled down over his longish hair.

'Best you turn around and head back to town,' he said when about twelve feet separated them. 'You're sure as hell not goin' anywhere else.' To prove that he meant it, he shifted the aim of his carbine so that it was pointed at O'Brien.

Ignoring it, O'Brien said, 'I want to see Haven.'

'That a fact?'

'I've got business with him.'

'What kind'a business?'

'That's between me and him.'

Scar-face looked him over. 'You carryin' any weapons?'

'No.'

'Step down a minute, let me make sure.'

'I told you—'

'Step down. You want to see Haven, we got to make sure you ain't carryin' no weapons first.'

O'Brien obeyed, leaving the mustang ground-hitched, and raised his arm. The other man also dismounted, booted his carbine and tied his mount to some brush, then came towards him.

O'Brien knew that word of the way he'd pistol-whipped the miner yesterday must have spread through Haven's men by now, and that the gun in the sling had lost whatever element of surprise it might once have had. What he aimed to do now was let them find what they wanted to find, and hope to God that they didn't search him any further once they'd found it.

Scar-face came up to him and looked him in the eye. He had soulless eyes, this man. There was nothing in them, only spite and brutality. He shoved one hand roughly into O'Brien's sling and O'Brien had to bite his tongue to stop from yelling at the pain that zigzagged up his arm.

He felt Scar-face close his fist around the .44. The man yanked the gun free and looked at it. 'Still want to see Haven?' he asked with a grin that revealed his crooked teeth.

O'Brien did his best to look disappointed that the weapon had been found and said, 'Yeah.'

'Well, you won't be needin' this now, will you?'

'I guess not.'

'All right. Mount up. I'll take you in.'

O'Brien let his breath out in a soft hiss of relief and swung back up into the saddle, feeling the cold but comforting metal of the hidden .38 digging into the base of his spine.

Haven's camp was a mile and a half further south and east, set out in a peaceful little glade beside the San Juan. As they crested a gentle rise and sent their horses down the far side, O'Brien took in the layout of the place.

About eight or nine tents had been set up with scant regard for order, conical bivouacs mostly, and in poor state of repair. A larger Sibley tent had been erected some little way off from the rest, with some fold-away camp chairs and a table set up out front. Smoke from a single cookfire at the centre of the camp trailed skyward to be whisked away on the warm wind, and O'Brien saw sunlight and steam sparkling off a pail of coffee suspended over the coals. A few men not on duty lounged or chatted in bunches in the central area. The ground around them was awash with empty, rusting cans. O'Brien counted a dozen or fifteen horses in a rope corral that had been rigged up near the river, where grass grew the juiciest. A stalled supply wagon stood off to the east.

As they approached the camp, some of the men began to sit up or turn around and watch them come. O'Brien tried to show them no fear. One of Haven's thugs stood up and ran toward the Sibley tent, and a moment later Alex Haven, 'Red Metal' Haven himself, strode out into the sunlight and stood with his fists on his hips, watching their approach.

O'Brien looked around the camp, searching for Gene Canfield, but Gene was nowhere in sight. Still, that was hardly surprising. After the beating O'Brien had given him yesterday, he was probably still laid up and licking his wounds.

The scar-faced man in the woollen cap led him in. It occurred to O'Brien that he must be about as welcome here as Thanksgiving on a turkey farm. Some of the miners reached for their carbines. He heard lever actions being worked and held his breath. At last they reined down before Haven, and Scar-face nodded and said, 'Caught him ridin' out of town, Mr Haven. Said he had business with you. I took his gun off him and fetched him in.' He took the pistol he'd taken out of O'Brien's sling from the waistband of his pants and tossed it down to the brawny-looking man who'd first alerted Haven.

Haven nodded without taking his half-hidden eyes off O'Brien. 'All right, Scott. Go back to your post now.'

Scar-face turned his horse with a deal more yanking and kicking than was required, and rode out. The man to whom he had thrown the .44 stepped off a few paces, but still lingered protectively nearby.

O'Brien regarded Haven from his saddle. Haven returned the appraisal without blinking. In daylight he looked a little younger than O'Brien's original estimate, though still well-advanced into his fifties.

He scratched thoughtfully at his hooked nose. He appeared tanned and weathered, with very long arms and legs beneath his black suit. He said, 'Is that right? That you have business with me?'

Uncomfortably aware of being the centre of attention, O'Brien said, 'Of a sort. I beat up two of your men yesterday.'

Haven's thick white beard moved slowly as he smiled, and saliva shone on his large, squarish, discoloured teeth. 'Yes. I wouldn't have believed it had I not seen with my eyes the sorry state in which they returned to camp. What of it?'

'Well, I got to thinking about it afterwards. I did what I did off my own back, Haven. I wouldn't want you to get the impression that them folks in Rock View put me up to it.'

Haven said, 'Now, why would I think that?'

'I don't know. You just might, that's all.'

'Wouldn't it be truer to say that the people of Rock View asked you to come out here and set the record straight? That they're afraid I will punish them for what *you* did?'

'You're punishing them already, aren't you?' O'Brien asked quietly.

Haven shrugged. There was a humidor on the little table beside him. He raised the lid, reached inside and took out a bloated Cuban cigar, which he then held to his ear and rolled. 'Do you have a name?' he asked suddenly.

O'Brien said yes he did, and told him what it was.

'Well then, Mr O'Brien. Since you seem to have fallen into the role of go-between, I'll give you a message you can take back to Munday and the others.

'I am not a novice in my field. I know my business just as surely as I daresay you know yours. I know how to read all the signs and indicators. I have made it my life's work. And unless I am severely deficient in all my calculations, I know almost exactly what I am going to find inside that mountain the citizens of Rock View hold so dear—a vein of copper one hundred feet long and six hundred feet wide. Do you know what that means?'

'Not really.'

'It means an annual yield of a hundred million pounds of copper *at least*. This year. Next year. Perhaps for the next decade.'

He put the cigar into his mouth and the brawny-looking man came forward again and thumb-scratched a match in order to light it. Haven drew deeply on the fragrant smoke, then took the cigar from his mouth and blew it out in a blue cloud. He said, 'Now, we can *all* make money out of this deal, if we're clever.'

'The people of Rock View aren't interested in making money.'

Haven's eyes glittered suddenly behind the pouches of flesh in which they sat. 'But I *am*, Mr O'Brien. And I fully intend to get it.' He said, 'I have been patient with these townsfolk you claim not to represent. I have waited with considerable restraint for them to come to their senses and accept the inevitable. But I am losing that patience, Mr O'Brien. Rapidly. And so are my men.' He gestured to them and the cigar in his hand left a trail of smoke in its wake. 'Look at them. How long do you think I can hold such a motley crew in check? Make no mistake about it—I have had my fill of waiting, and I will wait no longer. Either your friends in Rock View acquiesce, or I will grind them underfoot.'

'You won't get away with it. How can you?'

Again Haven smiled gently before plugging the cigar back into his mouth. 'It wouldn't be the first time,' he said easily.

'So that's what you want me to tell Munday and the others, is it? That you're losing patience.'

'No. I want you to tell them that I've already *lost* it. And one way or another, we will settle this business today.'

It was not so much a threat as a simple statement of fact, and that's what made it sound all the more ominous. Haven was always so blasted calm and confident that O'Brien wondered if anything could ruffle his feathers. 'Best you think twice before you do anything rash, Haven,' he advised, compelled to make at least some kind of response to the threat. 'I've talked to those people. They'll fight you every inch of the way on this. And if it comes to fighting, a lot of men'll end up getting hurt. *Your* men.'

But Haven knew the truth of the situation only too well. 'Come now, O'Brien. If you've spoken with the people of Rock View, then you know their attitude as well as I. They will fight us? They've got no fight in them, and they never did have. However...'

'What?'

'It is true that, if Munday fails to see reason, this business can only end one way—with violence. But there could be some kind of financial reward for the man who *makes* him see reason. Does such a proposition interest you?'

O'Brien shook his head. 'Not hardly.'

'Then you had better get back to Rock View and give them my message. I am not an ungenerous man. I will give them the better part of one more day. Munday can ride out here at any time, if he's prepared to sign the contracts and permits I've had drawn up. But if he isn't here by six o'clock this evening...we're coming in, and we're going to take over.'

O'Brien said, 'You're crazy if you think you can get away with that.'

Haven drew on his cigar some more. 'And who, pray tell, is to stop me?' he countered.

The drum of hoof beats disturbed the early-morning stillness just then, and O'Brien risked a glance over his shoulder to identify the newcomer.

Something dark and apprehensive wriggled around in his stomach when he recognised Ed Canfield, Gene's banker-twin brother, heeling a lathered mount in from the north. Immediately he transferred his reins from his left hand to the fingers of his right, to keep his surrogate gunhand free. Then he turned the mustang a little so that he would be facing Ed when Ed galloped in, and slowly he put his left hand behind him, ostensibly so that he could brace himself on his cantle, but in reality so that his hand would be that much closer to the .38 if he should need it.

Like the rest of them, Ed was no respecter of horseflesh. Great clods of earth flew up beneath his horse's pounding hooves as he sawed mercilessly at the reins, and the tails of his elegant Prince Albert flapped around him like bat's-wings. The resemblance between him and his brother really was remarkable. Each was a carbon copy of the other, save for their manner of dress.

Ed reined down about fifteen feet away, rage and hatred making little lights glow inside his black-brown eyes as his horse slithered to an ungainly halt.

'It's true what Scott said, then!' he snarled. 'You actually had the brass to show up here, after what you did to my brother!'

Haven said, 'How dare you leave your post! Get back there at once!'

But Ed was a man who seldom loved but hated often. 'Not until I've settled with this piece of trash!' he said, keeping his agate-hard eyes on O'Brien as he pushed back the flap of his jacket to reveal the butt of his New Line Police Colt.

'There'll be time enough for that before the day's out, unless I'm very much mistaken,' said Haven. 'For now, O'Brien is taking an ultimatum back to Rock View for us.'

Ed said, 'He's not going *anywhere!* You saw what he did to Gene. I'll kill him for that!'

O'Brien had been hoping he'd see reason. Like Haven said, there would be time enough later to settle whatever real or imagined scores existed between them. But Ed was having none of that. The bond between one twin and the other was too strong, and when one was cut, the other one bled.

So Ed went for his gun.

O'Brien saw his move and made one of his own. His left hand closed around the .38 and he pulled it out from beneath his jacket. Ed's Colt was just clearing leather when O'Brien shot him.

Ed twitched as blood surged from his left

shoulder. He cursed and the curse turned upwards at the end into a little scream. He swore again, his voice strengthened by rage, and carried on bringing the Colt up, and with no option, sweat popping like pearls on his forehead O'Brien shot him again, right in the chest, and this time an invisible hand scooped Ed backwards out of his saddle and deposited him into the dirt, where he lay spread-eagled on his back, absolutely still.

For a moment, the onlookers were frozen with shock. But O'Brien knew that wouldn't last forever, so he swung the .38 around on Haven. The Lightning was a double-action handgun. It didn't need to be cocked. But O'Brien cocked it anyway, for effect.

'Tell them to hold their fire!' he barked.

Haven looked up into the barrel of the gun, then beyond it, up, up into O'Brien's face. He stood very still for a moment, and for the first time O'Brien saw uncertainty in his expression.

'I mean it, Haven!' O'Brien said through set teeth. 'Any man here takes another shot at me and I'll kill you!'

Haven said, 'You haven't got the guts to shoot an unarmed man.'

O'Brien's lip curled. 'You want to bet on that?'

A moment passed. Lifting his voice, Haven called out, 'All right, men. Do as he says! We'll have no more gunplay!'

Another moment passed. Nothing happened. O'Brien looked down at Haven and wondered if he could actually clear this entire business up with just one more bullet. His finger tightened on the trigger.

But no. Haven was right. It wasn't in him to gun down an unarmed man. And he doubted whether Haven's death would necessarily solve anything. Without his controlling influence, these men would run riot on Rock View. And killing Haven now was as good as putting a gun to his own temple.

The big, brawny-looking man standing a few feet away suddenly threw the .44 to the ground. A couple of seconds later another man followed his lead, then another. O'Brien drew in a deep breath as the immediate threat of further violence faded.

'You still want me to take your message back to Munday?' he asked softly.

Haven nodded cautiously and spat out the cigar. 'I do,' he replied. 'Tell him that I can make life more unpleasant for him than he ever dreamed possible if he and his cronies do not bend to my will. Tell them that they have no option but to cooperate with me. Tell them that I have lost a good if impetuous man here this morning, and that my rage and the rage of this man's companions will only be assuaged by their complete and total compliance. Do you understand that?'

O'Brien nodded. 'I understand it.'

'Then you had best go now, while you still can.'

O'Brien glanced down at Ed's stiffening body. Blood had spread across his fancy brocade vest in the shape of a clenched fist. He looked up and over the surly-faced miners and thought, *Yes. I'd better go now.*

He reached down and took the reins

from between the fingers of his right hand. Then, jamming his heels into the animal's flanks, he got them out of there at a gallop.

EIGHT

O'Brien rode back to Rock View unchallenged, although he was sure that Haven's men, secreted in their hidden vantage-points, watched him every inch of the way. By the time he reached Main Street, the town was livelier than it had been when he'd left. He sent the mustang down the centre of the street and hauled in outside the stable, where he dismounted and led the animal inside.

Munday was beavering away over a ledger in his cramped little glass-paned office, and Eben was sitting on a barrel just outside the rear doors, whittling. They both looked up when they heard the clatter of horse-hoofs, and Munday threw down his pen and shoved away from his roll-top desk to come and greet him. His relief at seeing O'Brien was obvious, and when he was near enough, he had to fight against grabbing his hand and pumping it.

'O'Brien! God, man, I didn't expect we'd see you again so soon! I...'

He saw something in O'Brien's face that he didn't like the look of then, and some of the relief in him was replaced by more worry. 'What...' He swallowed. 'What is it? What happened out there?'

O'Brien said, 'I went out on a fool's errand, Munday. I tangled with Ed Canfield and had to kill him. But that wouldn't have made any difference. Haven had already made up his mind what he was aiming to do.'

Munday aged before his eyes. Clearing his throat he said, 'And...and what's that?'

'You've got until six o'clock this evening to sign his papers. If you haven't done it by then, he's going to come in and take over the town by force.'

Munday sagged a bit and whispered, *'No!'*

238

Irritably O'Brien said, 'Oh, come on, Munday. You knew it was on the cards, sooner or later. How else did you think this was going to end?'

Munday bristled at his tone. 'I'm on your side in this, don't forget.'

Eben came in from the back to join them, the stick and penknife still in his hands but forgotten now, as O'Brien said, 'I know. I'm sorry. But your people have got to make up their minds what they're going to do, and quickly, because six o'clock might sound a long way away, but it'll be on us before you know it.'

'What they're going to do?' Munday repeated. 'Surely, that's obvious. As head man, I'm going to have to sign Haven's papers and give him what he wants.'

'But that's not what you want to do, is it?'

'You know it isn't.'

Eben threw his stick into a nearby pile of hay and snapped his penknife shut. 'You decide to make a fight out of it, count me in. It's like O'Brien's woman said las' night. We got the best reasons in

239

the world to fight. An' sure enough, we're on our own in this.'

Munday grinned sourly with only one side of his mouth. 'We're certainly on our own. We can't count on getting much support for a fight from the others.'

'Then call them together and tell it how it is,' O'Brien counselled. 'Haven's backing them into a corner. The choice now is simple. They either put up or they shut up. If you can make them understand just how deadly this business is about to become, some of them might just decide to put up.'

Munday said, 'I *know* them, O'Brien. They'd need a good reason indeed before they decided to fight.'

'I thought they already had that—to stop their dead being shifted around to accommodate Haven.'

'I mean something more immediate, the kind of provocation even *they* can't ignore.'

'Seeing you getting beaten up yesterday wasn't enough, is that it?'

'Don't judge them too harshly, Mr

O'Brien. They're old, naive and scared. We all are.'

'And nobody knows that better than Haven. When he rides in, he won't be expecting a fight. That could be to our advantage.'

Munday said, 'Eben...'

'I know. I'll go get 'em. Your place?'

Munday nodded. 'My place. Meeting starts in twenty minutes.'

As Eben shuffled out, O'Brien said, 'Can I leave my horse with you?'

His mind obviously elsewhere, Munday said, 'Sure.'

'Thanks.'

'Oh, by the way. If you're planning to go find Miss Olsen, she's over at my house.'

O'Brien nodded.

He left his horse in Munday's care and headed for the hotel. Already he could feel tension growing in the town. Everywhere he looked he saw frightened people. Would they fight if it came to it, he wondered? He had a sinking feeling that they wouldn't.

He went up to his room, took out his gun, replaced the spent shells and slipped it back into his sling. Sitting on the edge of the bed, he looked out the window and wondered what kind of a fight they *could* put up. A bunch of old-timers who likely wouldn't know one end of a gun from the other and an ageing soldier of fortune temporarily denied the use of his gunhand. But what was the alternative? They had to try, at least.

O'Brien went back out onto the street and around to Munday's house. When his knock went unanswered, he went around the side of the little house to the backyard, where he found Mrs Munday, Laurel and Terry boiling washing in a big tub.

He watched them for a moment, Mrs Munday stirring the bubbling, soapy water with a stick, Laurel and Terry pegging shirts and sheets to a line, the three of them half-obscured by the rising, curling steam. It was such a commonplace scene that it was hard to believe that Rock View was actually a town under siege.

His eyes were drawn to Terry. She fitted in here with these people as if she had lived here all her life. The fact touched him, for she had never previously known what it was like to really belong anywhere.

He coughed to attract their attention, and Terry's blue eyes lit up and filled with tears when she saw him.

'O'Brien!'

She came to him and curled her damp hands around his good arm and squeezed. She asked him if he was all right and he said that he was. 'Your husband's called a meeting of the town council, ma'am,' he said, addressing Catherine. 'I think I might be a little early.'

'Not too early for some coffee, I suspect,' she replied.

'I'll see to it,' said Laurel. 'They'll all want some when they get here.'

'They might *need* it,' said O'Brien.

Mrs Munday's still-handsome face seemed to set like concrete. 'Bad news?' she asked gently.

He shrugged. 'This business is coming to a head,' he explained. 'Whether that's good or bad depends on how willing your menfolk are to fight to hold what's theirs.'

Terry led him inside just as Munday and a couple of the councilmen came through the front door. Eben fetched the remainder about ten minutes later, and at Munday's request, O'Brien told them about his meeting with Haven.

When he was finished, Frank the storekeeper jabbed a blunt finger at him and said, 'So you shot Canfield down deliberately, to spark off this showdown!'

'Now don't talk so danged stupid,' chided Eben.

'It's true! O'Brien wanted to cause trouble here any way he could! Well, he's certainly done it now!'

'You already heard what the man had to say. Haven'd made up his mind long before O'Brien did what he did.'

'Anyway, that's neither here nor there,' said Munday, brushing his fringe back off his forehead as he tried to bring order to the proceedings. 'The question we have to address now is this: what do we intend to do about it?'

'I suppose Mr O'Brien here is going to suggest that we fight,' said Doc Harper.

'To my way of thinking, you don't have much choice,' said O'Brien.

'It's not as simple as that,' said the tall, angular man in the black suit, glancing down at his pocket watch. 'We have a duty to protect our people. If we advocate the use of force, some of them might die.'

'And what's the alternative?' countered O'Brien. 'A living death under Haven's rule?'

'I say we give Haven what he wants,' said Frank. 'If we do that, he might go easy on us.'

Munday glanced hopelessly up at O'Brien. O'Brien shrugged and said, 'It's your choice to make. You already know what I think.'

The stable-owner glanced down at the carpet and wrung his hands. It was quiet in the room. After a time he looked up and said, 'We'll take a vote on it. All those in favour of putting up some show of resistance, say aye.'

Eben said, 'Aye.'

Munday waited a moment, hoping, but

the other councillors remained silent. At last he said, 'Aye.'

Doc Harper said in a hushed voice, 'Looks like we give in, then.'

Terry said, 'I'll fight alongside you if you want to make a stand, Mr Munday. Be proud to.'

All eyes turned to her but she didn't back down. If anything, her steely glare shamed them all.

Frank found his voice first. 'You?' he said. 'You're a woman.'

'I can handle a Winchester well enough, thanks to O'Brien,' she said.

'I'm willing to fight as well,' Laurel added impulsively.

'And me,' said her mother. 'We're not stupid, Frank. We can learn to handle weapons quick enough, if needs be. And we're not afraid to fight.'

Sensing a turning tide, O'Brien said, 'What do you say, Munday? You, me, Eben, the women. That's six.'

Munday's face was anguished. 'I appreciate the gesture,' he said. 'But... It's as I said last night, Mr O'Brien. I have to respect

246

the wishes of the majority.'

O'Brien said, 'And the rest of you men would still sooner give in than make a stand?'

No one answered, but in the circumstances that was answer enough.

He shook his head. 'Then you deserve everything you've got coming to you,' he told them softly. 'It's just too bad that you're going to drag all these other people down with you.'

'You're callin' it right again, young feller,' Eben muttered in disgust as he climbed sharply to his feet. 'Christ Awmighty, what's it take to get you folks to see sense? What's got to happen afore you'll say to hell with it an' do the right thing?'

Munday said, 'Eben—'

But Eben turned on his heel and stalked out, and a moment later they all heard the front door shut behind him.

There was some shuffling and clearing of the throat. A couple of the councilmen muttered some farewells and then they too got up and did a fine job of leaving without once looking at each other. O'Brien, Munday and the women watched them go, and finally Munday ran his fingers up through his hair and said heavily, 'Well...it looks like I'll be putting my John Hancock to Haven's papers after all. I'd better go saddle a horse, get it over and done with.'

'Be careful, Daddy,' Laurel choked.

He reached out and squeezed her arm. 'I will, honey, don't fret.' Then he looked at O'Brien. 'I'm sorry about all this, O'Brien. I know that, right the way through this, your only intention has been to try and help us. When Haven's men eventually ride in, it's going to put you in a bit of a fix, isn't it? What with the Canfield shooting?'

O'Brien only smiled. 'I'll cross that bridge when I come to it.' He stuck out his left hand. 'Good luck out there.'

'Thank you.'

Munday was heading for the front door when someone outside started thumping urgently against the panels. When Munday opened the door, the tall man in the black suit was standing there, slack-jawed.

'I think you better come quick, John,' he said breathlessly. 'It's Eben.'

'What about him?'

'He's talking wild, something about riding out and talking sense into Haven. He's fixed up a white flag and he's rigging out one of your horses right now!'

Without a backward glance, Munday pushed past the townsman and set off at a run. O'Brien, who had also heard what the townsman had to say, was right behind him.

They came out onto Main and started toward the stable. Eben was astride a fine charcoal grey out in front of the building, a creased and somewhat grubby white handkerchief impaled on a three-foot stick held in his free hand. Frank had hold of his reins and the pair of them were arguing, but Eben would not be swayed.

'Eben!' Munday called as he stamped up, breathing hard. 'What the devil do you think you're playing at? Haven't we got problems enough without you acting crazy as well?'

'Ain't playin' at nothin', John,' Eben said, looking down at him. 'But I sure as hell done me a heap o' thinkin', an' while I ain't never been what you might call a model citizen, might be I got a chance to do some good for the town now.'

'Don't be such a fool! Haven's all through listening to what we have to say! You ride out there and you could end up getting shot!'

'Under a flag o' truce? Get out of my way.'

'Eben—'

'Out of my *way*, dammit!'

He yanked the reins free of Frank's grasp and the charcoal sidestepped friskily, anxious to be on its way. Hurriedly the townsmen got out of its path. Eben jammed his heels into the animal and it took off at a hard run, leaving the rest of them there to watch him go, bracing his homemade white flag against one hip like a soldier with a guidon, the crumpled, soiled, sad-looking flag itself flapping and snapping in the slipstream as he left the doomed town behind him.

There was nothing to do now but wait, and as usual, waiting was the hardest job of all.

As word of the councilmen's decision spread through the town, the citizens retired to their homes to consider the consequences of their actions. Stores closed early. The boardwalks emptied out. The very life of Rock View seemed to evaporate in the nooning heat.

Munday and O'Brien did their waiting down at Munday's office. Munday was like a cat on hot bricks. He wanted to go after Eben and send him back to town. Now that his mind was made up, he just wanted to sign Haven's papers and be done with it, but Doc Harper and a couple of the others told him to wait a while and give Eben a chance. Eben was so crazy, they said with a forced and desperate kind of optimism, that he might just pull off some kind of a deal where the rest of them had failed.

An hour later someone spotted a horse coming in at a run and word filtered swiftly down to the stable at the far end of the street. O'Brien and Munday hustled outside and went to meet it at a wide-stepping, purposeful stride. Wrinkled, worried faces showed at every window, all of them watching for the newcomer's arrival.

Munday's eyesight wasn't what it might have been and he said, 'Can you make out who it is, yet?'

O'Brien couldn't, because the horse was still too far out. A few minutes later, however, and he confirmed that the animal was a charcoal grey, and that it was riderless.

No, not riderless.

Eben had been lashed belly-down across the saddle.

The animal had a good homing instinct, and once it reached the street it slowed and finally came to a skittish halt. O'Brien, fearing the worst, closed the final yards to the horse at a run, and the horse, unnerved by the sticky scent of blood and the buzzing of the flies attracted by it, showed him the whites of its eyes.

Some of the townsfolk came out of doors

to watch as O'Brien and Munday untied the bonds and slid Eben down off the saddle and onto the ground.

He was dead.

Munday gave a strange, strangulated sort of cry and brought his fisted right hand up to a spot between his eyes. He was still and quiet for five seconds. Then, suddenly, his shoulders gave a lurch and he sobbed, just the once.

O'Brien tried not to look at him, to give him some small degree of privacy until he could regain control of his emotions. As dispassionately as he could, he looked down at the whiskery old-timer. There was a single, deceptively small bullet-hole in his forehead, bluish around the edges and crusted black and red at the centre.

He reached down and closed Eben's glazed eyes, wondering what had happened out there at Haven's camp—assuming Eben had gotten that far. The old man wasn't a threat to anybody. But for some reason, someone had killed him.

Suddenly O'Brien frowned. The handkerchief Eben had used as his flag of truce had been stuffed into the old man's mouth. Grimacing, O'Brien took hold of one corner and pulled it out. A message had been written on the cloth square. He flattened it out on Eben's chest and read it.

His teeth clenched.

It said, NOW YOU KNOW WE MEAN BUSINESS.

By this time, Munday had gotten hold of himself, and seeing what had been scrawled across the handkerchief, he suddenly snatched it up and got to his feet. O'Brien squinted up at him as he in turn scowled at the people who had ventured outside.

'*Damn you!*' he cried. The wind sent dust-devils spiralling down the street. The only sound was the squeaking of a hinge somewhere not far away. 'They come here, they make our lives hell for all these months...they...they murder...Eben... They do *all* of this...and you still won't fight them?'

No-one, nothing, moved. Then—

Frank, the portly storekeeper, stepped

254

down into the street and came over, walking slowly, almost against his own will. He went right past Munday and looked down at all that was left of Eben, then rubbed a big, pudgy hand across his lower face.

Quietly he said, 'I'll fight with you.'

Another man on the boardwalk heard him and called out, 'Me too, John. I don't want to, but I see now that we got to.'

One by one, O'Brien watched them lift their hands or call out to show support and solidarity, and he knew that Eben's death had been the final straw, the one act of provocation Munday had spoken of that morning, the one deed that even these people could not ignore.

As the men of the town came out to look down at the body and declare their reluctant willingness to take up arms, O'Brien himself looked down at the old man. He heard Eben's voice in his head, saying, *What's it take to get you folks to see sense? What's got to happen afore you'll say to hell with it an' do the right thing?*

Had Eben also recalled what Munday

255

had said earlier that morning? Had he gone out to Haven actually hoping to provoke something like this? O'Brien found himself wondering if he had decided there and then at that final council meeting that he must sacrifice himself in order to spur his people into some kind of action.

What had he said just before he rode out? *While I ain't never been what you might call a model citizen, might be I got a chance to do some good for the town now.*

'I'll fight,' said another man in the crowd.

'And me.'

O'Brien thought, *Rest easy, Eben. You did some good, all right.*

'O'Brien?'

Munday's voice snapped him from his reverie. He looked up and said, 'What was that?'

Munday was palming tears from his cheeks. 'I said this is more in your line of country. There's an army here, waiting for orders. Tell us what we've got to do.'

O'Brien got to his feet. He looked at the sea of men facing him. There were about thirty of them. Terry, Catherine and Laurel were there as well. He said, 'All right. If you mean what you say, we'll give Haven hell with the hide off. But I only want the men who think they can take the strain. I'll leave it to Doc Harper to weed out anyone who's not up to the task.

'First thing the rest of you'll need are weapons. Good, reliable weapons. Once you've got those, and ammunition enough for what's to come, I'll want at least one man in every store or atop every roof along both sides of the street.'

'What about our women?' asked a man at the back of the assembly.

'They'll be out of harm's way down at the church.'

'How can you be sure of that?'

O'Brien's face hardened. 'Because Haven and his men're not going to *reach* the end of the street.'

Frank said, 'I got some guns in my store. They been there for a couple years, but they work fine.'

'All right,' O'Brien said with a nod. 'Pass them out. But before you get started, just hear me out, all of you.'

Again it went quiet in the street.

O'Brien said, 'It's no small thing to kill a man. What you're going to do today will give you nightmares for months to come, maybe even years. But you'll get over it. And one day you'll wake up and you'll be glad you did what you did, because you'll realise that as awful as it was, it was the right thing to do.

'Now get your weapons—there's a lot to do before Haven gets here!'

Something mischievous tampered with time and made it run at twice its normal rate. As a consequence, the afternoon fairly flew past. Those men Doc Harper adjudged to be fit enough were given guns and O'Brien saw to it that they were positioned where they would do the most good, in or above the stores lining Main.

The townsmen did as he told them quietly and without fuss, but he sensed in them an aura of fatality, and wondered if they would hold their nerve or break under fire. If enough of them broke, then this entire crazy plan would be over before it really got started.

But there was too much going on for him to dwell long on that possibility, and maybe that was why the sun appeared to be in such a hurry to reach beyond the western rims.

Terry and the Munday women were adamant about playing their part as well, and as much as he hated to put women in the front line, he couldn't afford the luxury of being able to pick and choose just then. So he assigned Catherine and Laurel to fairly well-fortified positions behind the false fronts of a couple of stores midway down the street, then ordered Terry to one of the buildings directly opposite.

She nodded her understanding but didn't go right away. Instead she looked up at him, and although she clearly was not looking forward to the coming action, there was no fear in her at all. As their eyes met, he saw only love in them, love for him, and he knew with some unpleasantness that he had been wrong about her, that she wasn't confusing love with gratitude or anything else, that she really *meant* what she felt for him.

She gave him a small smile and turned to go take up her position. He tried to decide how he really felt about her, but now was neither the time nor the place to ponder such a complicated issue.

At last it was all done, and Rock View lay still and silent, bathed in the deep amber-grey light of sunset. Haven would have guessed by now that Munday wasn't coming out to sign his papers, that he was committed to coming in and making good on his threat. But would he suspect a trap? It was possible. But he knew, or thought he knew, these people. He'd said himself that they had no fight in them.

Out front of the stable, O'Brien and Munday waited in edgy silence, O'Brien constantly scanning the basin and rims beyond the town through his field glasses. Very suddenly time seemed to slow down and drag. O'Brien took out his Hunter. It was five minutes to six.

He exchanged a loaded glance with Munday.

Six o'clock came and went. There was no sign of Haven and his men. But at six-fifteen O'Brien said quietly, 'Here they come.'

Munday, grown tired of waiting, suddenly perked up. 'What? Where?'

O'Brien held the field glasses out to him and said, 'Here, take a look for yourself.'

Munday put the lenses to his eyes and adjusted the focus a bit. A moment later he sucked in his breath and O'Brien knew that he had them spotted.

There were about forty hardcases in all, and at their head, imperious in his rusty black broadcloth, rode 'Red Metal' Haven. They were coming ahead in columns of two, just like the military, some of them wielding flaming torches, and they were probably the hardest, meanest-looking crew O'Brien had ever laid eyes on—which really was saying something.

Munday took the glasses from his eyes and turned to face his companion. Softly he said, 'We're not going to make it, are we? Our force against Haven's?'

O'Brien said, 'That's up to our force. If

261

they want their freedom strongly enough, if Eben's murder affected them strongly enough, then they'll *fight* strongly enough.' Munday offered him the field glasses back but he shook his head. 'I don't need them any more,' he said. 'Put them somewhere safe and take up your position, Munday. And good luck to you.'

Munday said, 'You too.'

O'Brien left him there and started down the centre of the street, feeling exposed as hell being so out in the open. But his presence here in the street was designed to serve a dual purpose: to tell his little army to prepare themselves because Haven was coming in, and to lure Haven himself deeper into the town, perhaps to speak with him. It was absolutely vital that they sucker Haven and his thugs right into town.

He no longer required the glasses to see Haven's force. They had descended the gentle slope to the south and were now coming in across the flats at a canter, their torches flickering and winking across the distance. O'Brien came to a halt about a quarter of the way down the street and waited for them, wondering whether this was to be an end or a new beginning.

The sun sank lower, the light grew that much poorer. O'Brien thought about Munday's limited vision. Would the rest of these old-timers be able to see well enough through the gloom?

He told himself to quit worrying, that it was too late for that now. If they were lucky, the fading daylight could work *for* them, as well as against them. And O'Brien's force had the element of surprise going for it as well.

He heard the low rumble of horse-hoofs and braced himself. Just beyond the town limits, Haven slowed the pace but kept them coming. Did he suspect anything? O'Brien kept telling himself, *No. No, you don't suspect a thing, Haven. just keep coming. That's the way... Come on, you bastards... Just keep coming...*

O'Brien saw Haven looking from left to right. The town was quiet. Too quiet. For one God-awful moment O'Brien thought that Haven, sensing a trap, was going to turn around and lead his men out of there, but still they kept coming. Now he saw Haven's face, his pouched eyes, the long, hooked nose, the thick white beard, saw that every man-jack there had fetched his carbine with him, even those holding their home-made torches.

At last Haven reined in twenty feet away and his men, strung out in a loose, ill-disciplined line behind him, also yanked their animals to a halt. For a while they just traded stares. Horses snorted and tossed their heads. Men eased their butts in the saddle or spat trail-dust off to one side.

Finally Haven said, 'Welcoming committee, O'Brien?'

O'Brien shrugged. 'I was the only one with guts enough to face you.'

'Did you pass along my message?'

'Uh-huh.'

'Munday didn't come.'

'No.'

'Instead there was an old man with a white flag. He had no authority to sign my papers so we shot him.'

264

'I know.'

Haven realised that this was getting them nowhere. The continued silence of the town was beginning to spook the men behind him, and perhaps it was communicating itself to him as well. 'Where is Munday?' Haven asked.

'At home, having his supper.'

Haven digested that. Then he said, 'Do you know something, Mr O'Brien?'

'What?'

'If I didn't know better, I'd think that this was some sort of trap.'

O'Brien reached up to scratch his ear. 'Do *you* know something, Haven?' he said. 'It is.'

As he said it, he threw himself sideways, thrust his left hand down into his sling and grabbed for his Colt. The world tilted crazily and he wondered for one fleeting moment whether the people of Rock View would back his play or not.

Then his fist closed around the .38, and he brought it out into the open and swung it up and around so that it was aimed right at Haven.

Haven's face registered outrage more than shock, but shock was there too. His face blanched and he roared some kind of a curse or an order, and behind him his men began to scatter like chaff in the wind.

O'Brien discharged his Colt at him but he was not a left-handed shooter. His aim was a little off and the bullet went wide. Haven's horse, however, came up on its hind legs and spilled Haven off its back and into the dust, where he lost his long gun, rolled onto all fours and began to scramble away from his attacker.

From within and atop the stores along both sides of the street came a sudden, withering volley of rifle and pistol-fire and O'Brien, crabbing sideways to get behind the cover of a seldom-used rain-barrel, got a brief, nightmare impression of searing muzzle-flashes and bursting smoke-clouds, but felt a surge of relief too, relief that, as old and scared and passive as they might be, the men of Rock View had risen to the occasion after all.

Suddenly the centre of the street became a battlefield.

As a second ragged volley thinned them out, some of the miners began struggling to turn their horses around and escape the cross-fire while others tried to bring their carbines into play and control their prancing horses all at once. A horse at the centre of the column grunted and slammed sideways, hurling its rider to earth with bone-crushing impact. Another miner screamed as a stray bullet tore into the meat of his arm and flipped him out of his saddle.

But Haven's men were nothing if not fighters. That's why they were on his payroll. Furthermore, they knew well the kind of enemy they were up against, and within seconds they'd started to organise some kind of retaliation.

A few hurled their torches at the nearest buildings, and though most just bounced off to extinguish themselves in the dust, a few struck their juiceless, weathered targets just right and fire began to spread up walls and across boardwalks.

Store windows shattered as lead punched through them. O'Brien took aim and fired another round into all the chaos. In desperation, a long-haired miner rode his horse straight up onto the boardwalk and fired his carbine into one of the stores as he blurred past. O'Brien thought he heard a scream come from inside the store, but maybe he imagined it. He watched the man come charging down the walk towards him, hunched down over his animal to avoid hitting his head on the porch above, then came out from behind the barrel and shot at him point-blank. His bullet hit the horse instead and the animal's legs went out from beneath it and it went down ass over tea-kettle, throwing its rider forward over its head so that he collided with and smashed right through a porch-post.

O'Brien saw men fighting their horses to a nervy standstill, bullets chewing up wooden boards or shattering plate glass. Another saddle emptied as a miner cartwheeled backwards into eternity. A horse whinnied and collapsed. Some of the miners, set a-foot now, threw themselves down behind the cover of the dead or dying animals and continued to return fire.

One of the miners sent his horse out ahead of the rest, maybe seeking escape that way. O'Brien saw his scarred face and recognised him as the man who had taken him to see Haven earlier that morning, the man Haven had called Scott.

Scott saw and recognised him hunkering behind the rain-barrel at exactly the same moment, and yanked on the rein to bring his mount to a halt. Clods of earth shot up beneath the animal's stiff legs as he jabbed the carbine in O'Brien's direction. The gun gave a crack and jagged splinters flew up from a board at O'Brien's feet.

He flinched instinctively and reacted the same way, firing the Colt in his hand, this time allowing for his tendency to shoot slightly off a-ways. Scott screamed as the bullet hit him in the left breast and pushed him off the far side of his horse to bounce and twitch dead upon the hardpack.

Someone screeched and fell out into the street through a broken store window. O'Brien slanted his gaze over at the dead man but couldn't identify him. He caught sight of Haven on the far side of the street. The mining engineer had regained his feet and was crouch-running back the way he'd come, reaching out his long, narrow arms to try and catch up a trotting, riderless horse.

O'Brien sighted along the Colt at him and depressed the trigger. The gun roared but the shot missed.

Haven heard or felt the bullet go close past him and gave up chasing the horse and turned instead, his thin, white-bearded face a mask of rage when he saw O'Brien on the other side of the street. In the next instant he spotted a carbine lying in the dirt in front of him and leapt for it. O'Brien made to fire another shot at him but two things happened at once: another riderless horse galloped past, stirrups and mane flapping wildly, which put him off, and his Colt clicked on an empty chamber.

When the horse was gone, he saw that Haven had moved a few yards further down the street in order to get a better shot at him.

Their eyes locked. There was no way for O'Brien to reload the Colt quickly enough. Haven slapped the carbine to his shoulder, sighted along the barrel—

Then, without warning, he twitched and yelled and crashed forward into the dirt and O'Brien, who'd felt certain that his number had finally come up, had to remind himself to release his trapped breath. He looked up onto the porch behind Haven, saw no-one, looked higher, up to the edge of the rooftop and saw Terry there, pausing in her deadly work to toss him a wave before working the lever of his Winchester again.

Another scream, close by. O'Brien twisted around but couldn't tell whether the sound had come from a wounded miner or a wounded townsman.

He fumbled out fresh rounds and started to reload. Thick black smoke was climbing into the air to cast a miserable grey pall across the street. Men were pawing at their smarting eyes and coughing as it clogged their throats. For one brief moment O'Brien's mind went back to Purgatory, to the night he had collared

Omaha Tom Barfoot, to the beginning of this whole sorry episode. He fired the reloaded .38 again and another miner slumped forward over his horse's whipping mane, crying out in pain.

O'Brien looked around the barrel and further along the street. Near as he could tell, a few stragglers had managed to escape. He couldn't tell for sure how many of them there were, eight, ten, twelve, something like that. The street itself was a battlefield littered with dead and wounded men and horses. It was impossible to estimate numbers with any accuracy, but from the extent of the damage that he could see, he knew that they had done what they'd set out to do—resist Haven and his bullies, and make them pay for what they had done to Eben.

The gunfire had faded to a few sporadic shots, which suited O'Brien, who had no desire to drag this business out to its inevitable conclusion. Lifting his voice he yelled, *'Hold your fire!* Everyone: *hold—your—fire!'*

It took some time before he could make

himself heard, but he kept at it and gradually the remaining gunfire petered out until all that was left was the soft crackle of the scattered fires and moaning of injured men and animals.

'You men out there!' he called. *'Have you had enough?'*

The whole town held its breath, waiting for Haven's men to give an answer. When no such answer came, O'Brien called, 'Come on now, you know the score! We've got you pinned down! We can hold you there all night, if we like. All tomorrow and the next day and the day after that, if we want to.'

'What's the alternative?' yelled a rough-voiced miner hunched down behind a dead horse seventy feet away.

'Throw out your weapons and give it up,' O'Brien called back. 'And no tricks. You'll each be searched for any concealed weapons. We've got a doctor here: he'll tend to your wounded if you cooperate.'

There was a pause. Then the miner yelled out, 'We got your word you people won't double-cross us?'

O'Brien said tiredly, 'You've got our word. And unlike you, we *honour* a flag of truce.'

Again they waited in silence for a reply. Still no immediate response was forthcoming. O'Brien reached up and wiped sweat off his battle-smudged face with the back of his hand, willing them to hurry up and reach a decision.

Suddenly someone threw a rifle out from behind one of the dead horses, and as O'Brien watched, one of the miners got up onto his feet and just stood there with his hands up. O'Brien told him to come on out, and for his friends to do likewise, and one by one, slowly, cautiously, reluctantly, that's just what they did.

It was over, he thought, though he could hardly believe it. The siege of Rock View was finally over.

Battle-weary, slightly stunned townsmen stumbled out of the stores and herded the prisoners down to the public corral, where their wounded would be tended by Doc Harper and they would all be held under guard until someone—O'Brien, most likely—could ride and fetch the authorities in from Mexican Hat. Munday came hustling down the street to organise a bucket-brigade to swamp out the fires. O'Brien watched him hustle past, knowing that his mind was still too preoccupied for the horror of what had happened here this bloody sunset to fully sink in.

He stood there on the boardwalk, watching some kind of order return to the town, and knew that in time everything would straighten itself out and peace and normality would return to this place.

Across the street, Haven stirred and groaned.

O'Brien went across to him, put a boot-toe under him and flipped him over onto his back. The man's pouched eyes were glazed and wandering, and he was moaning softly to himself. Terry's bullet had splintered his right shoulder-blade, O'Brien saw. He was in desperate pain, but barring infection he would live—live to stand trial for what he had done here, to this town and these people.

'O'Brien!'

He turned just as Terry came down off the opposite boardwalk and into the street, threw the Winchester aside and hurried towards him. He stood over Haven and watched her come, seeing once more the love in her eyes, the familiar flash of her smile, and wondering if what he felt inside him was love for *her*, deciding that—

A gunshot ripped through the sunset and wiped Terry's smile right off her face. Suddenly her expression became one of pained horror and she called his name again, but made it sound more like a scream this time. She staggered and collapsed onto her face, and for one timeless moment O'Brien just stood there, stunned, unable to believe the evidence of his eyes.

His lips worked soundlessly. *Terry.* Then something came up out of the pit of his stomach and he yelled, *'Terry!'*

Before he could go to her, another gun-shot crashed through the gloom. O'Brien saw the muzzle-flash from the edge of his vision and dropped to a crouch, where he heard the bullet thud into a store wall behind him.

Confusion mixed up his thoughts. His mind told him that this was over, that all the fighting and dying had ended.

Then he saw Gene Canfield on the other side of the street, Gene Canfield in his fancy cowboy Stetson and his crackling canvas jacket and his shotgun chaps, and something inside him snapped, for it was plain enough to see what had happened, that Gene had deliberately held back during the attack, just waiting for the right moment to strike and get even with the man who'd killed his brother.

O'Brien came up and extended the Colt before him and Gene, seeing him coming, knowing that he couldn't afford to stick around here any longer, not if he wanted to get out of there in once piece, turned and ran for a droop-headed horse further along the littered street.

O'Brien shot him once and Gene yelped and stumbled, one hand reaching down to his left calf, from which blood had suddenly erupted. He turned back to face

O'Brien and brought his Remington up, and O'Brien saw him do it and really didn't give a damn. He just kept striding across the street, Colt extended to arm's-length, thumb-cocking and firing, thumb-cocking and firing, saying, *'Bastard...you bastard...you BASTARD!'* over and over again.

Gene jerked and danced under the impacting slugs, still trying feebly to get away, but O'Brien was having none of that. He emptied the Colt into Gene and Gene's torso turned into a sieve as he lurched backwards and finally fell to the ground, where he rolled once, then died.

Only then did O'Brien return to his senses and turn to run back to Terry, feeling something sharp and deadly twisting inside him.

A crowd had gathered around her, Munday, his wife, his daughter, Frank, the doctor, some others. He shoved through them to get to her, pulled up sharp when he saw the crimson splash on the back of her shirt, dropped his gun, fell to his knees.

Slowly he reached down and turned her

over. She was limp and unresponsive. She was dead.

He looked down at her, feeling the muscles around his mouth jumping, his throat tightening. He ran his eyes over her thin, pale face. In death she looked hollow, just the way she'd looked the first time he saw her, at Habgood's place in Purgatory.

He pulled her to him, feeling the loose weight of her against his busted arm. Munday called his name but he paid no heed. There in the dying day nothing mattered to him save the one unalterable fact that she was dead. She was dead, and he never even got the chance to tell her goodbye.

O'Brien stood over the grave fifteen hours later, hat in hand, and let his faded blue eyes wander across the inscription on her marker.

TERESA OLSEN

'JOSEPHINE'

1863–1884

The morning had dawned bright and sharp, but now he could feel the rising sun on his back and he knew it was going to be another hot one.

He glanced up and across the cemetery. This business had started here. It seemed only fitting that it should end here as well.

His eyes paused briefly on the fresh, loose-packed mound of earth that marked Eben's grave a few yards away, then moved on to the men further up the gentle slope who were digging three more graves for the townsmen who had died in the fighting.

Then his attention returned to Terry's grave and when he muttered her name there was pain and longing and emptiness in his voice.

He heard footsteps behind him and glanced over his shoulder. Munday was coming up to join him. He watched the stable-owner climb higher, noting only briefly the blackened smudges of dead fires that scarred the town behind him. Rock View itself was silent, once more in mourning. Its people were hurting just as he was hurting. But the hurt would pass eventually, for all of them, and once it did, the repair work could begin.

At last Munday nodded a cautious greeting and brushed his fringe back off his forehead. 'All right?' he asked carefully.

'Fine,' O'Brien lied.

'You'll be on your way soon, I expect? To Mexican Hat?'

'Right this minute. You can't hold your prisoners in the public corral forever. Sooner they get taken in for trial, the better.'

'Oh, they're no problem. We hurt them, O'Brien. They're leaderless now, what with Haven being laid up, and demoralised.'

'Still...'

O'Brien looked back at Terry's grave and said softly, 'You know, she was the kind of girl who could've taught a lamp how to burn brighter.'

'Yes,' said Munday, swallowing softly. 'I imagine she was.'

O'Brien jammed his hat on his head and cleared his throat. 'I'll be moving, then,' he said, suddenly brisk and business-like. 'Expect me back with the sheriff in a couple of days.'

'I will.'

Munday watched him start back down the slope before something compelled him to say, 'She's not here, you know.'

O'Brien turned back to him with a question on his face, and Munday indicated the grave, feeling suddenly embarrassed. 'She's not here,' he said again. 'No more than our children are still here. She... She's gone to a better place than this, O'Brien. She's gone home. They all have. These graves, the markers...they're just our way of...well, commemorating them, I guess.'

Home. O'Brien thought about the word and decided he liked the idea that a girl who had always believed she never really belonged anywhere actually *did* have a place in the grand scheme of things, a place she *could* call home.

His chest was tight and he just wanted to be on the move. 'See you in a couple of days,' he said.

He went down to his waiting horse,

pulled the picket-pin and swung up into the saddle. He was just turning the animal away from the cemetery when a woman's voice said, 'Goodbye, O'Brien.'

He turned sharply, half-expecting to find Laurel Munday there, or Catherine, but there was no-one, just Munday himself far up the slope and, higher still, the townsmen digging the rest of the graves.

He glanced around, telling himself that his ears were playing tricks on him, telling himself—

A breeze sprang up and at the same time the voice whispered again, 'Goodbye, O'Brien.'

He sat the mustang a moment longer, head bent, savouring the sound of her voice one last time. At last he muttered a farewell of his own.

Then he touched his heels to the mustang, knowing that one day he would be able to remember her without feeling such a terrible mixture of grief and pain, but that it would not be for a long, long time yet, and rode out of town, headed for Mexican Hat.

This Large Print Book for the Partially sighted, who cannot read normal print, is published under the auspices of

THE ULVERSCROFT FOUNDATION